THEY CALL ME THE MERCENARY

#11

DEATH LUST!

Books by Jerry Ahern

The Survivalist Series
#1: Total War
#2: The Nightmare Begins
#3: The Quest
#4: The Doomsayer
#5: The Web
#6: The Savage Horde
#7: The Prophet

The Defender Series
#1: The Battle Begins
#2: The Killing Wedge
#3: Out of Control
#4: Decision Time
#5: Entrapment

They Call Me the Mercenary Series
#1: The Killer Genesis
#2: The Slaughter Run
#3: Fourth Reich Death Squad
#4: The Opium Hunter
#5: Canadian Killing Ground
#6: Vengeance Army
#7: Slave of the Warmonger
#8: Assassin's Express
#9: The Terror Contract
#10: Bush Warfare
#11: Death Lust!
#12: Headshot!
#13: Naked Blade, Naked Gun
#14: The Siberian Alternative
#15: The Afghanistan Penetration
#16: China Bloodhunt
#17: Buckingham Blowout

THEY CALL ME THE MERCENARY

#11

DEATH LUST!

JERRY AHERN

SPEAKING VOLUMES, LLC

NAPLES, FLORIDA

2013

THEY CALL ME THE MERCENARY

DEATH LUST! #11

ISBN 978-1-61232-225-4

For George and Clara Dreyer—a second set of parents to me all these years, and without whose efforts I'd have been a lonely man. Love . . .

Chapter One

Hank Frost opened his eye, looking out from under the brim of the slouch hat pulled low on his face against the glare of the desert sun. He rolled the Camel into the left corner of his mouth and inhaled deeply. He was hot, half-sleepy and bored. He noticed his lips felt hot—it wasn't the desert sun, but the burnt-out cigarette. He spit it into the sand a foot or so from where he sat under the modest shade of a fig tree.

There would be no peace for him—Frost knew that. Not until Eva Chapmann, the woman her own rogue mercenary band called "The Deathwitch," was dead. The one-eyed man had sometimes sought after other men deliberately to kill them, he reflected. As he had with Colonel Marcus Chapmann. This thing with Eva Chapmann, though—it was the first time he'd harbored a deathlust for a woman. A smile crossed his lips. It was the one thing he and Eva Chapmann had in common—a deathlust. He for her life and she for his. He laughed under his breath, doubting it would ever be something they'd discuss. The first chance he'd have, he'd kill her; however, wherever.

Frost was still stiff and sore from his last stint in the

hospital, after the attempt made on his own life and the life of Bess Stallman, his fiance? He loved Bess, wanted to marry her, but no matter how hard he tried he couldn't picture himself married.

Bess had been uninjured when the carload of gunmen had attacked on the all but deserted London street. Next time, Frost thought, he wouldn't be that lucky—they would get her. And him. He had sent Bess stateside to stay with Mike O'Hara, O'Hara, the FBI man, himself recuperating after hospitalization due to an earlier encounter with the Deathwitch and her men. Frost had decided long ago that in a strange way, O'Hara was just as committed to Bess as he was. And the one-eyed man could think of no one he trusted more than O'Hara to lay down his life for Bess if necessary.

Frost's time in the hospital had not been idle. Through Bess's wire service and newspaper friends and contacts of his own, Frost had learned of inordinately large arms purchases on the black market in North Africa. In one case, a blonde-haired woman calling herself Evelyn Charters had been involved. Frost had reasoned she had to be Eva Chapmann.

The arms purchases—assault rifles, machineguns, hand held rocket launchers, mortars and the munitions needed to make them work—spelled one thing to Frost. The Deathwitch was mounting a large, clandestine military operation, and somewhere in the Mediterranean. There were the historic conflicts in the Middle East, the relatively obscure conflict in the Sahara between the natives and the government. There was always Turkey, or Greece. Frost didn't know and no further information had come to him to provide a clue.

The one-eyed man lit another cigarette, spying across the blue-yellow flame of his battered Zippo a Land Rover, stirring a billowing cloud of dust in its wake as it approached the oasis. He assumed the man driving it or the man beside him, both wearing goggles to protect their eyes from the sand, would be Rene Armendez, the gunrunner.

Frost closed the cowling on the Zippo and dropped it in his jeans pocket. He stood up, his hat still low over his face. If the gunrunners dealt with Eva Chapmann, they could presumably have been told to be on guard for a one-eyed man. With the hat obscuring part of his face—he hoped—he'd have a chance to feel them out before they noticed the eyepatch.

He was sweating under the bush jacket he wore, but kept it on anyway. There was a Parkerized FN High Power, the barebones military model, stuffed in the waistband of his trousers, butt forward behind his left hip, the chamber loaded, the hammer cocked, the safety locked. He didn't think it advisable that the gunrunners—who would assume he was armed—know just where and with what.

The Land Rover stopped.

Frost mentally shrugged and undid the belt of the bush jacket, letting it fall open. In addition to the gun, in the small of his back, was clipped a Gerber MkI Boot Knife, and in his shirt pocket a last ditch back-up weapon. His friends at Armament Systems Products in Atlanta had gotten him something called "The Scribe." On the outside, it was a black cased felt tip pen. But once the cap was removed, rather than writing . . . Frost smiled at the thought, "The pen is

9

mightier than the sword," someone had once said. In this case, the pen *was* the sword—more icepick-sized but lethal nonetheless. It was a growing favorite among undercover types.

Two men climbed down from the Land Rover now. Frost didn't know which one was Rene Armendez. Both had nearly identical builds, were dark-haired and dark-complected and covered with desert dust.

"You are the American who wants night vision devices for Libya?"

Frost nodded. He'd needed a cover story and the Libyans were always trying to buy black market arms products which legitimately they couldn't purchase. It was an obvious cover story, but he hoped so obvious it would sound real enough.

"Can't you talk?"

It was the nearer of the two almost identical men, the one who'd spoken the first time. Frost searched their faces and builds. This one, the one who had spoken, wore his watch on his right wrist—left handed then, the one-eyed man noted.

"I can talk—when I got somethin' to talk about," Frost almost whispered.

"You want these pieces of equipment?" The man was left handed. Frost could see him edging his left hand toward his belt, to get closer to a gun.

"I don't—the Libyans do." It was true—the Libyans were looking for a new night vision camera surveillance system.

"I talked with one other man—he too wanted these."

"You know how the Libyans are," Frost smiled. "They know they can't buy used G.I. toilet paper

10

legitimately—they put out a lot of feelers. It's the classic joke in the arms business—always has been last ten years or so. Libyans from London."

"Are your principals from London?"

"Yeah," Frost lied.

"I don't believe you."

"I don't care," Frost smiled, watching the left hand as it inched closer to the open coat.

"I think you are a policeman—maybe."

Frost cocked his hat back from his face with his left thumb. "Ever see a one-eyed cop?"

"One-eye—then you are not a policeman."

Frost let himself smile. He knew the left-handed man and maybe the other half of the bookend set had made him. It sounded like something from a comedy mystery or a 1940s flick, he thought—beware the one-eyed man! They'd met Eva Chapmann. "You guys know little Eva?" Frost smiled.

"What is this?"

"Eva Chapmann, Evelyn Charters—whatever. The Deathwitch. You know her?"

"What if—"

"You were right—I don't want anything for the Libyan Government—except maybe a timely end. I want something for me." Frost lit another cigarette.

"Then you are a rich man," the left-handed man nodded. "A night vision surveillance system as you mention—it is expensive."

"I'm nervous about burglars—live in New York. You know how that is," Frost smiled.

"The big banana?"

"Apple," Frost smiled. "What about it?"

"You are a liar—or a policeman—but I don't think either maybe."

"What do you think?" the one-eyed man asked.

"This Eva—she mentioned a man. A man with one eye."

"Nice to know she was thinking of me," Frost smiled again.

"She said you should be killed if you were ever seen."

"You planning to follow her advice?"

"I think so," the left-handed man said, starting to edge away from his friend.

Frost eyed both men, knowing what they planned—get on his flanks and open up. He slowly stooped down into a crouch over the sand. "Too hot to fight, guys," Frost laughed, glancing once over his shoulder at the two Arabs who'd driven him into the desert—they worked for Rene Armendez and would fight with him. Four men, Frost thought.

One of the Arabs was edging a curved-bladed knife half out of a metallic sheath—Frost could hear it as well as see it.

Frost's left hand snatched a handful of sand. The one-eyed man hurled it toward the left-handed man—Armendez? Frost's right fist gripped the butt of the FN High Power 9mm, his thumb wiping off the smallish safety catch, his trigger finger already starting to pump.

Armendez was screaming, swearing, a pistol firing into the dirt where Frost had been, but Frost rolled now, across the sand, his own pistol firing once, then once again, cutting down the man beside Armendez as he drew a bright nickel plated Government Model Colt auto. The second man spun, plopping back against a palm tree and hugging his arms around it, the .45 booming once as, dead already, he skidded down along the trunk into the sand.

The Arab with the long curved-bladed knife was coming at him and Frost snarled, "Eat lead, sucker," firing the High Power in a fast, two shot burst. Both slugs impacted high—Frost thought it was the angle he fired from on the ground. The first hit the Arab's throat near the adam's apple, the second into the open mouth.

The Arab fell forward, carried by his own momentum, blood vomiting out of his throat and squirting from his neck.

Frost rolled aside as the body flopped into the sand, the body bouncing up as a slug impacted against it. Frost rolled. It was the second Arab, a revolver in his left fist, his right thumb cocking it. "Dummy," Frost snapped, shaking his head, firing the High Power again. The Arab arced back like a felled tree, two holes in his chest, the revolver firing into the air as he went down.

Frost started to turn—Armendez. But Armendez was firing his pistol again, the sand beside Frost's left arm exploding upward. Frost swung the muzzle of his High Power on line as Armendez made to fire again.

But the automatic in Armendez's left hand was jammed. The French Moroccan looked up from the gun and into Frost's face, the one-eyed man laughing. "Drop it, asshole."

Armendez threw the pistol, like a movie cowboy, Frost thought, Frost dodging aside, the gun skidding into the sand.

"What now?" Frost almost laughed, stuffing his own pistol, safety upped, into the waistband of his jeans.

Armendez said nothing, but twisted his left arm in some sort of complicated, almost cat-like movement, a long bladed, spear point knife sliding down into his palm.

"You really Armendez?" Frost smiled.

"Yes."

"Good—otherwise I'd shoot you instead of this foolishness." Frost's right hand snaked behind him, to the Gerber MkI boot knife in the sheath in the small of his back, the catspaw surfaced handle under his curled fingers.

Armendez was already coming at him and Frost sidestepped, the boot knife snaking out as his right arm snapped forward in a straight arm thrust, his right foot going out to trip Armendez. The point of Frost's blade caught on Armendez's shirt, ripping away half the sleeve, but there was no blood Frost could see as Armendez went down. The French Moroccan rolled, tossing up sand toward Frost's face, duplicating Frost's earlier ploy. The one-eyed man dove left and to the ground, his legs scissoring around Armendez's right arm, then releasing. Armendez was already rolling, to slash at Frost with the knife in his left hand. Frost pushed himself up on his hands and the toes of his feet and threw himself across the narrow expanse of sand separating them. Armendez had completed the roll, belly down now in the sand, the knife in his left hand flailing as Frost fell across his back.

Frost's left fist grabbed at the knife hand, pinning it by the wrist, his right hand driving forward, stopping just shy of the point of his boot knife penetrating Armendez's neck just below the right ear at the jaw line. Frost, his breath short, rasped, "Let your knife go or I'll cut off your ear."

Armendez tossed the knife and Frost, without moving his, kicked Armendez's knife across the sand. The one-eyed man thought a moment as he sat across Armendez's back, not moving the knife. Now that he had Armendez, what was he going to do with him?

Chapter Two

Frost lit a Camel, and as he did bent his head to look with his good right eye over the rims of his sunglasses at the other patrons of the bar. A smile crossed his lips, his salt and pepper stubbled cheeks creasing with it. If he'd been looking to get knifed, mugged, robbed or something similar, it would have been the perfect place. He stuffed the half empty pack of cigarettes into the left outside pocket of his rumpled white suit, dragging heavily on the cigarette and almost simultaneously exhaling the gray smoke through his nostrils.

Frost glanced at the black faced Rolex Sea-Dweller on his left wrist and the rank of empty glasses on the rough wooden table in front of him—he had been in the bar two hours. He picked up the half drained glass of scotch and took a swallow. Bar whiskey in a place like The Seafarer's Oasis would have been worse tasting than the scotch and twice as deadly.

The one-eyed man swallowed hard, the medicinal-smelling liquor burning slightly as it went down his throat.

Armendez, after the knife fight, had taken Frost across the desert to the "sales floor" for Armendez's arms business—a large oasis near a deserted village burnt out in a firestorm three years earlier, Armendez had grunted. There had been seven Arabs working there, sorting through crates Frost recognized as stolen U.S. M-16s. With a pistol to his head, Armendez had ordered the Arabs away, toward the gutted village.

Frost had then simply asked one question of the French Moroccan with the Spanish sounding last name and left-hand dominance. Cocking the hammer of the High Power and holding the muzzle under Armendez's nose, Frost had only repeated the question once.

And because of that, Frost thought, he now sat in what could easily be labeled a North African waterfront dive. Eva Chapman's latest arms shipments were going out that night on the ship of Captain Evan Kruger, the Liberian registry freighter *The Cyclops*. Frost laughed at the thought—a one-eyed man seeking information about a ship named after a one-eyed humanoid monster of mythology. The coincidence amused him. Frost sipped at his drink. The next coincidence did not amuse him.

Several men walked through the batwing doors leading to the back bar from the restaurant filling the front room of the structure. One of the men was a one-eyed man, as was Frost. Their builds were similar, Frost noted, and the man's hair was dark and he needed a shave, as did Frost. And the one-eyed stranger was talking animatedly with Rene Armendez.

"Should have killed that sucker," Frost rasped to himself.

"What?"

Frost looked up from his table, trying to avoid

Armendez seeing him, recognizing him. There was a burly man, teetering drunkenly, leaning across toward Frost, his hands resting on the far edge of the rough wooden table behind which Frost sat.

"Huh?"

"What were you saying? " the man grumbled, his breath almost making Frost's cigarette flame even at the distance.

A fight in the bar would perhaps keep Armendez from spotting him, and the one-eyed stranger who had come in with Armendez — it had possibilities, Frost thought.

Frost looked up at the hulking man opposite him, the man looking like a stage seaman, in red and white horizontal striped shirt, beer and grease stained. "I said you're some kind of pussy whip," Frost smiled.

The man's brow knit, the eyes becoming tight black dots. "What is this catwhip."

"No — pussywhip — see," Frost smiled patiently, explaining, "that means you're — well . . . Let's start over again." Frost had noticed the man's accent as French. "Comprendez-vous schlemiel?"

The man shook his head negatively.

Frost held up the first finger of his left hand a moment, signalling pause while he thought. Finally, "Let's just say, I don't like your face, think your mother was very ugly and your father had homosexual relations with a grapefruit." Frost smiled.

The big man snarled and reached across the table. Frost wondered if he'd made the right move.

The big man's hands started for Frost's throat, Frost hammering his left fist toward the man's jaw. Frost's left connected and nothing happened, the hands starting to close around Frost's neck. Frost hammered forward with his right, the table splintering in front of him as the big man seemed to almost walk through it. Frost's right slammed against the man's jaw, catching it at the tip, Frost feeling the skin of his knuckles splitting. The fingers were tightening around Frost's throat.

Frost hammered both fists inward, slapping them against the big man's rib cage. Still the fingers tightened around his throat. The fingers of Frost's hands splayed as he brought his hands up toward the man's face, the tightness in his throat making red and yellow and gold floaters pass before his eye. Frost's fingers moved against the face, his thumbs digging into the big man's ears, his fingers searching out the eyes and nose, twisting, tugging, tearing at the face.

There was a scream, like a bellow from a wounded animal and the pressure around Frost's throat stopped, the one-eyed man sagging to the floor, coughing, choking.

The big man screamed again and Frost, on his knees, straight-armed the man with his right, pounding against the man's crotch. He could feel the testicles squish as his fist impacted. The big man screamed this time, but a higher pitch, more a real, human scream, the hands grabbing for the crotch as Frost fell back.

If blood could fill an eye, Frost thought, this man's eyes were filled. He started toward Frost. As Frost hauled himself to his feet, he could see Armendez, pulling a pistol from his belt, hear Armendez shouting, "Get him!"

Frost pulled the FN High Power from under his

coat and fired twice, Armendez's head exploding under the impact of the 110-grain JHPs. The big man was still coming even as Armendez spun and fell toward the bar, blood spattering from the head.

Frost leveled the gun in his hand at the big man, the big man never hesitating, still coming for him. The sensible thing, Frost knew, would be to empty the remaining eleven rounds in the High Power, empty them into the big man with the red and white striped T-shirt. But it wasn't the big man's fault Frost had needed a fight and picked him to start it with. Frost let the big man come, then hauled his right fist back and up, the High Power still in it, crashing the pistol forward in a long diagonal sweep, the one-eyed man's wrist almost breaking as the pistol connected with the left side of the big man's neck. The big man tottered back on his feet, swaying, Frost executing a half right turn, lashing out as he did with his left foot, the flat of his sole catching the big man square in the solar plexus, doubling him forward. Frost rammed the pistol into his belt, still with no desire to kill the big man, his fists balling together, hammering down hard on the big man's neck.

The big man went down.

Frost felt a tug at his shoulders and, instinctively, dodged and ducked, a fist flying forward, over him, slicing the air. Frost's left elbow hammered back, the one-eyed man hearing a groan, a heavy sigh as he twisted all the way left, his right balled fist cutting straight forward, into the face of the man who'd been behind him — another seaman, probably off the same ship, Frost thought.

The fighting in the barroom was general now,

chairs crashing down on heads, tables splintering as bodies lurched against them or on them. Frost dodged right, another fist coming his way, his left punching out low into the gut of one of his faceless opponents. He sidestepped, a chair splintering onto the wall behind where his head had been. His right foot flashed foward, the toe catching a man with a green shirt and a blue watch cap, the man doubling forward, Frost grappling at the shoulders, hammering the man's body and head against the wall where the chair had broken.

One of the men who'd walked into the bar with Rene Armendez and the one-eyed sailor was in front of Frost now, a bottle in his right hand. Frost ducked, the bottle slicing air, Frost's right straight-arming foward, crushing the man's nose under it, the man falling back.

There were two men fighting three feet to Frost's left and Frost started past them, wanting the one-eyed man. Both men stopped fighting as Frost started by, shouting something in a language Frost couldn't understand, turning toward him, lunging for him.

Frost blocked a right haymaker with his left forearm, took a half step forward on his right foot and thudded a right cross into the man's jaw, ducking as the man to his right swung for him, Frost lashing out across his body as he spun, Frost's left tipping the second man on the jaw, the second man sprawling back across one of the few still unbroken tables, the table crashing to the sawdust covered floor.

Frost shoved a smallish man aside, the man coming at him with fists flailing but no definite fighting style. He started toward the bar, the one-eyed sailor there fighting with two men and holding his own. The smallish man came for him again and Frost wheeled, feigned a left, sidestepped and crossed the man's jaw with his right, the man going down.

Frost stepped over an unconscious man with blood trickling from his nose, then ducked a bottle and connected a right uppercut to the man with the bottle's jaw, then reached the bar.

The one-eyed sailor had backed off the taller of the two men he'd been fighting but the shorter of his opponents, a man with a gray splotched full beard, was coming at him with a knife. Frost started for him but too late, the knife connecting into the one-eyed sailor's right kidney. Frost's right fist hammered out, Frost outreaching himself, falling behind the blow, his fist connecting hard with the left temple of the shorter man with the knife, knocking him back, Frost half sprawling across the bar.

Frost pushed himself to his feet, the man he'd hit in the temple still holding the blood-dripping switch-blade knife, staggering toward him, the taller man closing in on Frost's right as he turned, his back against the bar. He pushed himself up, using the bar as leverage, his right foot snapping out, catching the taller man square in the throat, the man stumbling back, gagging.

Frost flung his own body over the bar, flipping it, landing on his feet, the knifer reaching out, Frost's right fist hammering down on the knife hand forearm, pinning it across the bar top for an instant.

He found a bottle with his left hand and swung his arm with the bottle almost like an extension, but awkwardly because of the length of the reach, the bottle crashing down on the left side of the knifer's head, Frost turning his face away as shards of glass and a spray of cheap whiskey washed across him.

Frost's left hand grabbed at the knifehand wrist, wrenching it back against itself, breaking it as the knife skittered across the bar. Frost let the knifer go, slithering across the bar and dropping from sight. He flipped the bar, blocking a swinging right with his left, stepping into his anonymous attacker, hammering his right fist into the solar plexus, then crashing his left fist down and across the man's jaw.

The man stumbled back.

Frost dropped to a crouch. The one-eyed sailor was still breathing, but blood dribbled from his mouth and it wasn't from a cut, Frost realized. He picked the man up in a fireman's carry, letting him drop across his left shoulder.

The big man, the sailor in the red and white striped T-shirt was coming at him, hurtling the still fighting men to each side as he charged like a rhino.

Frost pulled the FN High Power and shoved it out at arm's length, shouting in English, hoping the man would understand, "I don't wanna shoot you—but so help me—"

The big man stopped in mid-stride, shrugged his shoulders and grabbed at a standing body off to his left. He punched the new victim hard in the face and let the body drop to the floor.

He shrugged again, "Oui!" Then he started away.

Frost shoved his pistol in his pants and carried the one-eyed sailor out into the restaurant, through the batwing doors, police sirens in the distance. Frost noticed that the man across his shoulder was dead.

Chapter Three

"That was one hell of a fight man, huh?"

Frost looked across the small cabin and at the black man who'd made the remark.

"Yeah—sure was."

"Hey, Gardner," the black man persisted. "Who started that fight?"

"Damned if I know," Frost answered. "I was walkin' in with Armendez and those others. Never saw."

"Me neither—funny." The black seaman got up, nodded once and walked out.

Frost leaned back against the bulkhead and sighed hard. It so far had been less than an efficient operation. First, he'd decided not to kill Armendez in the desert, then had to kill Armendez anyway hundreds of miles away while following up the information Armendez had given him, Amateurish, Frost decided, still chastizing himself. Then the bar fight. The one-eyed sailor he'd changed places with now had died before Frost had been able to get him to talk. Consequently, Frost had no idea who the man knew abroad the freighter and who he didn't. Did the captain know him well? What was the man's nickname? Frost had read the sea papers, knew the formal name—Marcel Gardner. Frost doubted the guy ran around letting himself be called Marcel—it sounded too much like something women did to their hair.

Frost checked the Timex he'd taken from Gardner—in five more minutes he'd be on watch. As he stood up, he felt the Rolex in his trouser pocket—and he felt the FN High Power under his shirt. It was actually Gardner's shirt, out of his seabag which had been stowed aboard the ship. Frost had changed clothes with Gardner in the alley, then dumped the body over the wharf side. Fortunately the half naked, identification-devoid body had not surfaced in the six hours it had taken waiting to get out of the harbor on the morning tide. The seabag, other than fresh clothes, had offered nothing of value. Gardner had smoked marijuana—that was in the seabag. But since Frost didn't—he had enough troubles with drinking—the MaryJane was of no interest. Gardner had liked to read porno novels. Frost didn't object to that at all, but the problem was they were in Spanish. Frost didn't read it well enough to understand the dirty words.

The seapapers and all other documents in Gardner's wallet had indicated he should be English speaking, so Frost had gambled and so far not been caught. The first night out eating in the galley, someone had remarked, "I always heard you liked red peppers, Gardner—from Jamie Pinch. Too hot, these ones, huh?"

Frost had shrugged and eaten one of the red peppers, then another and then a third. He had spent the first hour he'd had off watch in the head and his stomach still didn't feel right.

So far, there had been no nickname and no evidence anyone aboard the crew knew Marcel Gardner intimately or well enough even to know one one-eyed man from another. Frost wondered if that was what bothered his stomach, more so than the peppers.

There was one man aboard the ship—Frost had heard references to him—who had shipped with Gardner once before, a man named Amos Fleiger. As left handedly as he could, Frost had gotten a sufficient description of Fleiger to be able to recognize the man at least. But Fleiger always liked working the dogwatch and until this morning—the third day out of port—Frost and Fleiger hadn't crossed paths. But Frost had decided to change that, out of necessity, trading watches with one of the three men he shared a cabin with, the black man who'd just left, Algernon Wingo—"Nonnie" as everyone called him.

Frost checked the stolen Timex again. It was time to go. He grabbed up the Greek seaman's cap from Gardner's things and started out into the companion-way. It was empty, Frost intentionally making himself late. He wasn't going directly to his watch, but to Fleiger's watch instead.

And under his shirt, as he walked, Frost felt for the butt of the little boot knife—he thought he might need it.

Thunderheads rumbled off in the distance toward North Africa, he thought, as Frost found the forecastle where Fleiger should be standing his watch. Fleiger rode the forward deck gun which had been installed just after leaving port. Frost wondered if that elevated Fleiger from ordinary seaman to a gunnery officer. He mentally shrugged, eyeing the shadow of the man leaning by the jack staff in the prow of the ship.

Frost started forward, glancing from side to side, seeing no one. The man in the prow by the bow pulpit turned suddenly and Frost stopped moving. The man moved slightly, starting forward. Frost couldn't see the face yet, but knew it was Fleiger. When Frsot heard the voice. "Gardner—that you?"

Frost coughed and grunted, "Yeah—figured to see ya."

"You ain't Gardner, one-eye."

Frost shrugged his shoulders and started walking forward again. "No—but ain't ain't good English."

"Who the fu—"

"Hey—let's talk," Frost murmured, not wanting to kill the man but seeing little other choice for himself if he wanted to stay alive aboard the ship.

"Who are you? You kill Gardner?"

"No," Frost answered honestly. "There was a bar fight. Gardner was goin' after two guys and I started over to help him out—figured one-eyed men should stick together. Anyway, I wanted to talk to him. Wouldn't talk much dead. He got a knife in his kidney. I hauled him up over my shoulder to get him out of there and he died by the time I got through the door."

"Then you switched places with him."

Frost just nodded, not really knowing if Fleiger could see the movement or not in the shadow.

"Why—what'ya want? You some kinda Fed?"

"What—me?"

"The guns and shit we got on board for that Chapmann dame?"

27

"What do you know about that?" Frost asked, stopping now, less than a yard from Fleiger.

"I know the captain's gettin' a ton of money for haulin' 'em and that crooked bastard Rene Armendez suppplied 'em."

"He won't supply anything else to anyone," Frost added.

"Kill him too?"

"What's with the 'too', huh? I didn't kill Gardner—I told you that."

"Yeah," Fleiger groaned. "Just some kinda coincidence you and him lookin' so much alike and all, right? Both with one eye. That really a bad eye or just part of some God damn disguise?"

"Pal—if this could be a disguise," and Frost sidestepped into a yellow running light's glow, lifting away his eyepatch.

"Jesus!"

"Yeah," Frost murmured, putting the patch back in place. "I used that name a few times myself when it happened."

"How'd you lose the eye?" the man asked.

Frost felt a smile creasing his cheeks, his lips upcurving slightly. "Well, not much of a story really," Frost began. "I used to pal around with this guy named George—real clumsy. Well, George and I were havin' this game of pool, you know. He was on one side of the table, I was on the other. Well, George was makin' this bridge shot. Well, see, George was near sighted and hated to wear his glasses. I was bendin' over the table to see what was takin' him so long. Guess he saw the white of my left eye and—well, thought it was the cue ball. I don't wanna talk about it," and Frost tugged at his eyepatch.

"Bullshit," Fleiger rasped.

Frost shrugged. "When you been without an eye as long as I have, the jokes get harder and harder. You should hear some my old ones. I was pickin' my nose, sneezed and my finger slipped. Then there's the one about a game of strip marbles with a tribe of cannibals, then—"

"Why'd you come up here?"

Frost shrugged again, deciding to be honest all the way. "To figure out if I had to kill you. I need a line on Eva Chapmann—tried killing me, tried killing my woman. I gotta pull the plug on her before she does it to me. It's a long story."

"I don't wanna hear it. Ain't none of my business."

"There you go," Frost smiled, "using ain't again."

"You better try and kill me—cause otherwise I'm gonna kill—"

He never finished the sentence, Frost jumping back as the edge of a Bowie knife sliced through the air inches from his throat, the steel unreal-looking in the yellow of the running light. Fleiger came in after it, the knife in his right hand like a swordsman holding a rapier. Frost dodged to his own right, Fleiger having to twist off balance to swipe the blade at him.

Frost's own knife was out, the little Gerber's blade half the size of the Bowie and from the sound the Bowie made as it sliced the air, half the thickness too.

Fleiger overreached, Frost sidestepping again, but this time into the knife arm, chopping down with his own blade at the exposed inside of Fleiger's right elbow.

Frost could feel the blood spurting toward his face

29

as he half wheeled, ramming his right elbow back, hammering it against Fleiger's chest. The seaman fell back, the Bowie knife clattering to the deck. Frost wheeled, starting toward him, but Fleiger, his right arm streaming blood was coming at him again, some kind of rope in his left hand, swinging wildly over his head and on the end of the rope a round, huge metal disk—a rat guard, Frost realized, ducking.

The rope with the rat guard swung over him, connecting against the rail. Frost threw himself toward Fleiger before he could recover the rope, Fleiger's left hand gouging at the one-eyed man's face, the fingers digging at Frost's right eye. Fleiger was laughing. Frost rammed his little knife forward, hard, feeling the rush of air hard against his face.

Frost pulled the knife and rammed it forward again, Fleiger's grip on his face loosening.

The seaman who could have betrayed him fell back off the knife, Frost sinking back heavily against the rail, looking down at the dark blackness of the water and the tiny white, almost iridescent lines of foam there in the wake of the bow.

He squinted hard, his eye burning, but he guessed not permanently damaged.

He'd have to weight the body—maybe use the rope and the rat guard as a start, then swab the deck with something to get the blood stains. Maybe the captain and crew would think Fleiger had fallen overboard. Frost understood Fleiger drank heavily. Maybe an emptied bottle of whiskey on the deck would be enough to make it look convincing. Frost sighed hard, before turning to start the task. "Ohh—" He glanced at the borrowed Timex on his wrist. It was just after twelve midnight. "What a way to start a day," the one-eyed man murmured. Then he turned around and started moving the body.

Chapter Four

"Hey, Gardner—hey, man?"

It was Nonnie, and Frost looked up from his plate of bacon and eggs and across the table at the black man. "What?"

"I think somebody killed Fleiger—that's what I think."

Frost shrugged. "Hope not," he added. "Don't want somebody runnin' around the ship who likes to kill people."

"You was askin' about him," the Chinese at the far end of the table in the ship's galley asked.

Frost looked over at the man. "Yeah—I was. So?"

Frost took a swallow of his coffee, listening. "So, nothin', maybe, then maybe somethin'."

"What'd the captain ask ya?" Nonnie murmured through a mouthful of eggs, some of the too-yellow-looking eggs, yellower-looking against his dark skin, edging out the corner of his mouth.

"Same thing he probably asked you," Frost remarked. "Wanted to know if I knew Fleiger—told him I did back a while ago but hadn't seen him so far since we'd been out. Stuff like that."

"I hear we make the rendezvous today—fourth day

out," the Chinese at the end of the table remarked. Frost almost felt like kissing him for changing the subject. Since Fleiger's death had been discovered at seven that morning, there had been no end to the round of questioning and speculation. Frost glanced down at the Timex on his wrist, the Rolex still in his pocket. It was eleven thirty and the first chance anyone aboard ship had had to eat. There had been the questions about going back to the ship's approximate position to search for Fleiger, but that had gone by the boards—the captain had to make his rendezvous. As Frost judged it, another ship from one of the other coasts would meet them. And likely, the one-eyed man thought, the Deathwitch, Eva Chapmann, would be aboard.

The Mediterranean, with its shores abutting both Europe and Africa and political persuasions from the mundane to the bizarre, was like a back alley in a tough neighborhood, Frost thought, smiling as he took a piece of bread to sponge up his eggs. Everyone and anyone could meet somewhere in the middle and exchange smuggled goods, illicit arms, drugs—the possibilities were endless and the Mediterranean had been that way for millenia.

Frost pushed himself up from his plate, backstepped over the bench and started to get rid of his plate. He froze, a claxon sounding, shrill, unmistakable. Aboard a naval vessel—he'd been on one or two over the years—it would have been sounding general quarters.

But here, the one-eyed man knew better. It would be Eva Chapmann's ship, come to fetch the smuggled munitions. The Deathwitch. For some reason he couldn't understand himself, as he lit a cigarette in the blue yellow flame of his Zippo, he realized he was smiling.

Chapter Five

"Dammit!" Frost drew his left hand back away from the rough wooden crate marked "Agricultural Spare Parts," sucking at his first finger as if trying to extract snake venom. There was a splinter in his hand. He looked across the crate, down now on the deck, the box split open when it had fallen. It hadn't been intentional, to drop his end of the crate and let the contents burst out, but now that it had happened, he wasn't sorry. You could tell a great deal about the goal of a clandestine operation by the weapons used. In Viet Nam, "sanitized" weapons made to match those of the enemy were standard for some operations.

Rene Armendez, the gunrunner he had killed, had told him back in the desert that Eva Chapmann had purchased M-16s. But she had not. The guns in the case were FN-FALs like those carried by many of the NATO nations. Frost plucked the splinter from his finger, gave his skin a quick look to make certain it was all gone, then sucked at his finger again as he bent to retrieve the guns.

The FN-FALs were stolen, Frost decided, or at least counterfeited to look like they belonged to one of the NATO nations. The legends showed them as British

Army issue. The smaller boxes, Frost decided, would be pistols, much like his own—9mm FN High Powers.

There were boxes too that were made of cardboard, much lighter to carry. These would be uniforms—and Frost realized these would be British as well. British uniforms and guns. The British Army had been more talked about since England flexed her muscles in the Falkland Islands dispute, but talked about or not, the average British soldier was as good a fighting man as any in the world.

"England," the one-eyed man murmured. "Mumph ..."

"What you say, Gardner?"

It was Nonnie, the ship's only black seaman.

Frost shrugged as he packed the last of the assault rifles into the battered crate. "Just wondering out loud why these things are English," Frost answered.

"To match the amphibs and shit captain brought out last trip. But this is all, I guess."

"Ohh," Frost murmured, boosting the crate again. "Amphibious landing craft?"

"You got it," then Nonnie went on, carrying two of the lightweight cartons.

Eva Chapmann was aboard, the thought making Frost's skin crawl. All she had to do was see him and it was pull leather and die, he knew. He'd go for the High Power sweating against his abdomen and try to kill her, her men killing him. Frost wondered if he died, would O'Hara take care of Bess for him. Frost figured his strange FBI friend would. Frost hefted his end of the box and started walking, the Chinese opposite him.

Frost could see her on the bridge, talking with the captain, her blonde hair all but obscured with a dark gray bandanna, her perennial UZI submachinegun slung under her right arm.

He stopped walking, staring.

"Hey—the captain will get—"

"The captain can get fucked," Frost rasped, setting down his end of the case; the Chinese looked perplexed.

"You crazy!"

"Get Nonnie and yourself someplace fast—I got somethin' to do."

The Chinese looked at him, the one-eyed man letting a smile cross his lips. "You and all the other guys suspected it—I'm not Gardner. And I killed Fleiger. But only when Fleiger tried killing me. That woman up there, the one talking with the captain. Her name is Eva Chapmann. She tried murdering me after trying to blind my good eye, left me in the jungle for animal bait. She tried dumping the Space Shuttle all over the middle of Manhattan just for revenge against the United States. She tried killing me and my girl in London, put me in the hospital. Her guys got into a firefight with my best friend and nearly killed him. Now she's trying to start a God damned war with this stuff. She's gonna die and there's gonna be shooting—a lot of it. You and Nonnie get to a lifeboat or something."

"Lifeboat?" the Chinese repeated.

"Yeah—couple tons of explosives in the hold—I'm blowin' 'em. Alert the captain and I'll drill you too."

The Chinese took a step back. "What's your name?"

"Frost," the one-eyed man smiled. "What's yours?"

"Tsung—Fred Tsung."

"Then get out of here, Fred."

The Chinese started to move, then turned around. "If I leave you here with the crate, the captain'll spot it for sure—you get under that tarp with it, huh."

Frost nodded, wondering about the man, then hefting the crate again. Starting to walk again, the Chinese murmured, "You gonna kill yourself, you know?"

"Maybe," Frost nodded. "Got no choice— she's gotta die, got tight security around her all the time and from the looks of this stuff, I don't have much time."

"Hey," the Chinese said, reaching the shelter of the tarp, the shadow sharp contrast to the burning sunlight. "Me and Nonnie get that—" and Tsung paused, two of the other crew members passing them. "You know—that," Tsung murmured, Frost guessing he didn't want to say lifeboat. "Hey—we got enough oars to go around for three, huh?"

Frost set down his end of the crate, looking into the man's dark eyes, the squint around them. It wasn't the sun, but a smile. "Thanks," and Frost clapped the Chinese on the shoulder and started from under the tarp.

The Chinese walked just behind him toward the hold, but as Frost entered it, Tsung cut left, away from the hold. Frost thought he caught sight of Nonnie on the portside deck railing, Tsung going toward him.

Frost ducked his head, starting down the narrow metal rungs into the main cargo hold. There were men down there still, and so were the explosives. Frost didn't really have much of a plan, he realized, simply to set the explosives with some kind of improvised time fuse, then get back topside and shoot Eva Chapmann, then shout for everyone to abandon ship, that it was going to blow.

He made it to the base of the hold and started aft, toward where the explosives—plastique and conventional explosives—were stored. Most of the heavy stuff was being brought up on the ship's elevators, but Eva Chapmann had ordered a spot check of the equipment before handing over her money. Most of the weapons and explosives were now aboard the elevators, ready to be brought topside when Eva handed out the cash, Frost judged.

There were three men beside the elevators, he recognized them as some of the more insistent questioners about his possible involvement in the death of Fleiger earlier that day.

"Whatd'ya want, Gardner?" the taller of the three men snapped.

"Captain wants you guys topside—told me to run the elevators up."

"Bullshit," the tall man snapped.

"Get topside," Frost murmured, his voice low.

"Go to hell, fella," the tall man responded.

Frost shrugged, started to turn and wheeled around, the FN High Power snaking out in his right fist. The tall man started to move, Frost snapping, "Don't—I'm gonna blow this stuff—now get out of here."

"Some kind of fuckin' cop! Shit—you can—"

Frost could only see it as a blur, something smashing down toward his gunhand, then felt the pain across his right forearm, the High Power falling from his suddenly numbed fist.

38

Frost saw another blur, the tall man going into action against him. He sidestepped, half wheeling, his right foot snapping up, kicking toward the tall man's face, missing, a stubby man with no shirt and a massive beer pot throwing himself toward Frost. Frost wheeled again, his left foot lashing out, catching the stubby man in the gun, then Frost wheeled again, his right foot impacting against the taller man's chest, driving him back. Frost started to wheel, feeling hands on his shoulders. The one-eyed man rammed his left elbow back, feeling it connect against something soft and sweaty. Frost felt the hands on his shoulders go limp as he wheeled again.

It was the third man, half doubled over, but his head low and charging. Frost snapped his right foot up, the instep catching the third man at the tip of the jaw, the balding head snapping back with an audible cracking sound.

The tall man was coming again, and Frost half turned left, the tall man's right foot, then his left foot, then his right foot coming in a wheeling attack.

Frost caught the left leg, Frost's right fist straight-arming into the tall man's crotch as the one-eyed man ducked, loosing the block against the right leg, letting it swing over him as the tall man stumbled away.

The half naked man with the beer pot was coming again and Frost backstepped; a chain was in the man's hands. He was swinging it like a flail and Frost dodged, backstepping again. The beer pot man was recovering the chain for another swing and Frost started to backstep again, but felt the bulkhead at his back. As the chain swung down. Frost hit the deck, the chain snapping against the bulkhead so hard Frost could see the sparks of metal frictioning against metal.

Frost scissored out his right leg in a sweep, connecting against the man with the beer pot's knees. The man started to fall back. Frost was on his hands now, shifting his body weight to the toes of his left foot, scissoring his right leg out again, hammering his foot against the man's crotch.

The man with the beer pot screamed, falling back against the opposing bulkhead, the chain clattering to the floor.

Frost looked up, the tall man coming, with a fire axe high over his head already on the downswing. He rolled, half slipping on the greasy deck as he pushed himself up, the chain the beer pot man had dropped in his fists. As the axe swung down, Frost snapped the chain wide between his fists, catching the axe at the center of the handle, deflecting the blow. The one-eyed man wheeled hard left, hauling the chain hard over his right shoulder, the axe skittering to the floor, bouncing once, the tall man's body half over Frost's right shoulder. Frost let the body slide back, rose to his full height and rammed his right elbow back, once to the solar plexus. Frost took a half step back, glancing over his right shoulder as the tall man doubled over behind him, then smashed back with his right elbow again, turning his face away as the man's shattered teeth and blood from his lips spurted outward.

Frost wheeled 180 degrees, then wheeled hard right, on his right foot, his left foot stomping out, Frost's left fist hammering forward into the crown of the tall man's head.

Frost backstepped, the beer pot man coming at him

again. Frost wheeled half left, away from the man, Frost's right foot snapping out, the full force of his heel catching the beer pot man in the throat.

The man fell, like the tall man, dead.

Frost picked up his gun, sucking in his breath. He found the third man—dead also.

The elevator was loaded. Frost found the switch, like a power main switch. He felt a smile cross his lips, shaking his head, sweat streaming down from his hair and dripping from his mustache. He pulled the little Gerber from his belt and started to strip the already exposed wires. Then all that would be needed would be a fuse.

Once he activated the elevator switch, the spark would ignite the fuse and it would only be a matter of time.

As he worked, he glanced over his shoulder—there wasn't fuse, but there was twine and it would burn. He guessed his time would be three minutes or less—to get topside, shoot Eva Chapmann and then abandon ship. The one-eyed man didn't think he'd make it, at least the last part, the part about getting off the ship.

Chapter Six

The one-eyed man pulled the elevator start switch by the topside entrance down then started up out of the hold, onto the deck, the sun blindingly bright and yet seeming cool to his body after the dank and stagnant air of the hold. He shivered slightly, half from the sweat drying against his bare arms and under his shirt, half with the understanding of what he was about to do. He glanced at the Rolex on his wrist, thought of Bess for a second and smiled. He started across the deck, Chapmann men with UZI sub-machineguns everywhere, inspecting open crates of assault rifles, British uniforms—almost absently, Frost wondered what the Deathwitch had been planning. There were two Chapmann men at the base of the steps leading up to the bridge where Eva herself stood, in easy sight.

Frost glanced at the Rolex again. Maybe a minute or two on the fuse. He had packed it so that after igniting with the elevator switch from the electrical spark, the fuse would be lost inside the packing crates themselves and couldn't be blown out by the wind. The elevator doors were already opening, causing commotion at the center of the deck amidships.

Stopping less than two yards from the two UZI armed guards at the base of the steps, Frost reached out his left hand, the Timex in it, then joked. "Hey—either one of you guys stand a good deal on a hot watch?"

One of the men to Frost's right started forward a step, swinging his UZI back out of the guard position, reaching out for the watch. Frost dropped the watch to the deck and grabbed at the man's right wrist, jerking the man forward, off his feet, Frost's right hand already holding the FN High Power. Frost pumped the trigger twice, catching the second man in the face, then twisted the pistol to his left and down, pumping two fast shots into the head of the first guard, the man already stumbling to the deck.

Eva Chapmann wheeled, screaming something Frost couldn't make out. Frost leveled the FN High Power at her head, shouted, "Die!"

He pumped the trigger twice, but already knew it had taken too long. She was moving, dodging to her right and Frost's slugs ripped through her left shoulder and into her chest. Her Uzi was firing and Frost felt something tearing at his left side. He spun, started falling toward the deck.

The one-eyed man grabbed up the Uzi from the dead man beside him and rolled onto his back, firing toward the bridge. But Eva Chapmann wasn't in sight.

"There's a—"

Frost guessed the last of the shouted words would have been bomb, or maybe fuse, but Frost never heard the word as the deck shuddered hard under him and his ears rang with the concussion. He felt his body hurtled up off the deck and falling down again, his nose crinkling at the acrid smell of the explosives and the oil and gas. Frost felt the heat searing his skin, opened his eye and realized he was less than a dozen yards from the fireball, still soaring skyward.

Frost shoved himself to his feet, the Uzi gone, as was the FN High Power. There was a pain in his left side and he touched his left hand to it, feeling the stickiness of his own blood. He stumbled ahead, the deck rumbling again under him. Frost fell forward. As the ringing started to die in his ears, he could hear other noises, louder seeming though he knew they really weren't, and terrible. It was screaming, men afire, mostly Chapmann men, running, submachine-guns firing wildly into the air, into the steel plate deck, bullets ricochetting, whining as they impacted against the metal.

And over the starboard rail, Frost could see Eva Chapmann, in a small launch now, held up by two of her men, the left side of her short sleeved bush jacket drenched with blood, but the Uzi still in her right fist.

Frost lurched against the railing as there was another explosion. Men were jumping overboard to quench the fires consuming them, screams dying as they splattered against the water, the water around the boat starting to steam.

There was a groan and Frost slid left, toward the bow of the ship. The freighter was already starting to the bottom.

And now he could see Eva Chapmann, standing, shaking but standing on her own, see her mouth moving but not hear the words. "Alive!" The word came from Frost's contorted mouth like a curse.

44

He started forward, holding the rail as the ship lurched beneath him. The deck gun. He didn't recall the make, or the type really either, but somehow knew that once he got the breech open and a round loaded, none of that would matter anyway.

He stumbled, his face whacking hard into the steel deck plates, feeling his nose bleeding, his lips cut.

"Bess," the one-eyed man murmured, glancing absently to the face of his Rolex.

There were still Chapmann men aboard as Frost lurched his way forward, one of them seeing him he realized, shouting, "Kill him!"

Frost snatched at his little knife, his right hand arcing out, hurtling the knife underhand, planting the blade half to the hilt square in the center of the man's chest.

Frost lurched away from the rail, gabbing for the dead man's Uzi. He had it now, spraying toward a concentration of Chapmann men trying to flip over the side into the water.

Frost dropped the empty gun as the last body bounced and fell. He started forward again toward the deck gun. He glanced right once, over the rail. Eva Chapmann had one man helping her as she started up from the small launch toward the deck of her yacht. "Alive!" Frost threw himself the last few feet, wrestling away the tarp covering the deck gun. There was a metal box, and Frost wrenched the box lid up, wondering why with his luck the box lid hadn't been locked. He grabbed one of the rocket shaped rounds for the deck gun, stuffing it under him as he sank into the seat behind the breech.

He found the breech latch and wrenched the action

open, inserting the round and closing the breech. There was a bullseye shaped rear sight and he lined the front sight up to it, then settled on the yacht.

Frost's fingers found the firing mechanism and he worked it, the roar of the gun temporarily deafening him. He could see the smoke trail as the deck gun impacted off the port bow of Eva Chapmann's white yacht. There was a dark stain there now, but the one-eyed man could see the ship wasn't seriously damaged.

He bent to snatch up a second round as the deck guns aboard the yacht opened up. One of the guns was firing toward him. Frost could feel the deck under him shudder as a round impacted nearby, shards of white hot metal raining down.

The one-eyed man covered his face with his hands, then started again to load his second round. The other deck guns aboard the yacht were firing into the water at the white boats splotched across the whitecaps. She was murdering any witnesses, Frost realized, whether her own men or the crewmen of the freighter.

Frost had the deck gun loaded and swung it on an arc, toward amidships of the yacht. He worked the firing mechanism, the roar now just a dull thud to him, his hearing so blunted he couldn't feel the ringing anymore.

The white yacht was hit—he could feel it before he saw it, knowing the shot had been right.

But the yacht's deck guns were still firing.

There was a small, elevated helicopter deck aft on the yacht and as he squinted hard through the sweat and dirt and maybe blood—he didn't know—that streamed down his face, he could just discern the blonde hair, the scarf that had bound it gone, the hair blowing in the wind of the fires amidships of the yacht as Eva Chapmann made for the helicopter.

"No-o-o!" Frost felt the word rather than heard himself say it. He reached down for a third round for the deck gun, clearing the breech, ramming the fresh round home and securing the breech.

There seemed like plenty of elevation on the gun. He'd fire at the helicopter, he reasoned.

His feet were wet and Frost looked down, the bow already partially awash, water swirling around his feet now and washing inside his shoes.

"Kiss your tuschie good-bye," the one-eyed man rasped, elevating the gun as the helicopter started airborne.

Frost fired once. His heart sank, the elevation too poor, the helicopter too fast, the hit a clean miss.

He could almost make out her face in the bubble domed helicopter as it spun over him.

He raised his fist, then the middle finger of his hand toward her. His hearing was starting to come back a little and vaguely, he could hear the pounding of metal against metal as the subgun fire from both sides of the chopper started.

He could see the water churn, pieces of metal deck plate fly, then felt the hits ripping against his flesh as he sank forward across the deck gun.

He tasted salt across his lips, not knowing if it were ocean water, blood or tears—tears that Eva Chapmann was not dead, tears for the world—the one-eyed man closed his eye, the sea water cool against his face. . . .

47

Chapter Seven

Bess was holding his head against her abdomen, rocking him, telling him he was going to make it. He felt like laughing on the inside, saying something to her about it, but he couldn't talk. "Can't talk," he told himself, then opened his eye.

He closed his eye, wanting the image back, but it was gone. As Frost opened his eye again, he knew the origin of the rocking—a lifeboat.

There were two faces looking down at him, one black and one with a yellowish cast. He tried to speak, but realized his mouth was dry. Nonnie bent over him, elevated his head and poured water into his mouth. Frost started to feel himself choking, but swallowed some of the water.

"You're shot up pretty bad, man—but you maybe gonna live as long as we do. And that ain't too long."

Frost tried to smile, tried again to speak. This time his voice worked, but not well yet. And he suddenly realized he could hear again. "Thank you."

"Shit man—you the one told old Tsung there we should get our asses into a lifeboat. You saved our lives, even if ya did blow up the fuckin' boat on us."

"Who—ahh—what hap—" Frost wanted a cigarette. "Got a smoke?"

"They was a little wet but I dried 'em—here," and the black man propped Frost's head against the gunwales, Frost feeling something rough, a kind of cloth behind his neck. A blanket? The black man lit the cigarette with the lighter—it was Frost's own Zippo. "Neither one of us smokes—but figured if you woke up again, you'd be hungry for one."

The black man placed the tip of the cigarette between Frost's lips—he could feel them swollen, thicker than they should have been.

"What—"

He almost dropped the cigarette but Nonnie put it back in his mouth for him.

It was Fred Tsung who spoke. "That devil lady shot you out from behind the deck gun, but her yacht was goin' down and Nonnie and me figured her deckgunners would be too busy tryin' to save their own skins to notice us. So—anyway, we went back. No big thing, you know. That chopper of hers was gone and the deck was pretty much awash so it—"

"You could have died—both of you." Frost groaned.

"Yeah—I hope you appreciate that, man," Nonnie smiled.

Frost laughed—"Yeah—real good I appreciate it. We're adrift together so we'll die together rather than separately."

"You got it," Nonnie nodded, the smile gone. "Sharks—got them I dunno what kind but I betchya they ain't vegetarians. And we got enough water for about two more days. You been out sixteen, eighteen hours so you missed yourself a lot of the good part.

There was a storm last night."

Frost glanced at his Rolex, then squinted at the position of the sun. It had to be just past dawn of the next day.

"Any idea where—"

Tsung cut him off. "Yeah—middle of the Mediterranean—can't be too much more specific though. I don't think we're anywhere near the regular shipping lanes. Captain wouldn't have risked that with the cargo we was carrying."

"You ever been shipwrecked, Fred?" Nonnie asked the Chinese.

"No."

"Me neither—and I don't think I'm gonna be again."

Frost glanced to his left—his neck hurt badly as he did. Stiffness he guessed.

He felt the cigarette taken from his lips as his eye started to close. But the last image he maintained was a dorsal fin—knifing across the water. . . .

Chapter Eight

Frost felt the lifeboat rocking as he opened his eye, heard Nonnie screaming. Tsung was shouting in Chinese and Frost couldn't understand it. The sky was purple off to his right as the one-eyed man, stiff, his left side paining, his mouth dry, started to try and push himself up.

Nonnie was holding something in his hands, cursing, hammering it down into the water.

Frost rolled over onto his stomach, pushing up on his hands. Nonnie was bending too far over the gunwales and Tsung was starting up, the boat rocking.

"Look out, Fred," Frost shouted to the Chinese, but suddenly the boat was moving, rocking, starting to tip and water splashed Frost's face and inches from him now over the partially awash bow of the lifeboat he could see a gaping mouth.

"Shit!"

Frost heard the scream and realized it was him, punching out with his right fist into the deck and rolling himself back as the jaws of the creature closed, wood splintering around him.

And now Frost could see Nonnie, like a harpooner

51

after a whale, driving what looked like a spiked boat hook into the head of a massive gray-colored writhing thing in the water.

He knew the creature and it made him feel nauseated—shark.

The boat was lurching violently now and Frost rolled· again, more of the gunwale splintering as another of the creatures attacked.

"Nonnie!" Frost heard himself shout as the black man hurtled himself forward against the shark, Tsung reaching after him but grabbing air as Nonnie vanished over the side.

Tsung stood stock still, the boat swaying violently under him and Frost could see in the purple light tears streaming down the Chinese's cheeks.

"Nonnie!" This time the shout was Tsung's, but there was no answer. The lifeboat stopped its rocking. Frost looked to his right, where the lifeboat shipped water through the chunks ripped from the gunwales by the shark. He saw something floating on the water—a human leg, the skin dark against the darker water.

Frost lurched up into a sitting position and wanted to throw up but there was nothing in his stomach. His stomach rolled though—heaving. He half fell forward as he tried getting to his knees, to get Tsung down from his precarious standing position in the lifeboat.

"Nonnie!" Tsung shouted again. "Non—"

And Frost knew Tsung had seen the leg as well. Frost couldn't understand the words—Chinese again, but somehow he knew what they meant as Tsung stepped over him, half stumbling, taking one of the oars and beating it into the water.

The lifeboat started lurching again as Frost tried grabbing for Tsung, but then the boat twisted, almost shooting upright, Frost sinking, sliding across the rough wooden planking toward the holes in the gunwales, Tsung pitching over the side as the boat rolled, Frost flopping into the water, the boat over him, his head aching suddenly and badly but he didn't know why.

Frost reached out with his hand, his left side burning, stinging with the salt water and the pain. He hauled his hands out from under the lifeboat, drawing them back suddenly as a chunk of the lifeboat was ripped away, then another. Frost edged back, the lifeboat righting itself, Frost's head banged hard against it.

He was in the water, the lifeboat flopping half awash less than a yard from him. To the far side of the lifeboat the water was churning and Frost knew what it was—Tsung and a shark.

Frost swam toward the lifeboat, one of the oars still anchored into one of the locks. He started up into the lifeboat, reaching for the oar handle, twisting it out of the lock. Frost drew it inside, water up over his ankles, the boat rocking as he stood.

"Fred!" Frost shouted toward the churning water. "Fred!"

He used the oar like a staff to get himself to his full height, then raised the oar, swatting it down toward the dorsal fin twisting through the churning white water. The churning stopped, the fin arcing hard away from the lifeboat.

Frost could see bits and pieces of the Chinese, still floating on the water, and the dorsal fin streaking toward the lifeboat.

He raised the oar again. "Die you mother—"

There was a shot, then another and another and more than two hundred yards behind him, Frost could see a shape, his eye blurring. He turned around, ignoring it, swinging the oar toward the shark again as it came for him. There was another shot as Frost swung and the water churned, the fin lurching.

Frost couldn't help himself, falling after the oar, the weight of it carrying him over the side.

As he hit the water he saw a yellow tinged human ear floating beside him and heaved into the salt water, passing out. . . .

Chapter Nine

Frost opened his eye. He tried to move, but there was a stiffness in his left side. He opened his mouth, the lips not feeling swollen. Something smelled and he turned his face to his left, for the frist time noticing the pillowcase under his head. The smell was some kind of flower—subtle, yet definite and not unpleasant.

He looked down across the length of his body, seeing the gray hairs of his chest mixed with the black just below the nipples of his breasts the top of a dark blue floral print sheet. He tried to raise his head, found that he could and felt encouraged enough to sit up.

As he sat up, he banged his head into something and looked up above him—there was a bunk folded out of a cabin bulkhead. He could feel the motion and now looking around him realized it was in fact a ship. He was in the lower berth.

The sheets, the way they looked and the smell puzzled him.

Frost swung his legs over the bunk and put his feet on the floor, looking more closely at the bandage on his left side. It was neat, clean, looking as though it had been changed recently.

Frost glanced at the Rolex. Unless the date adjustment was wrong, two days had passed since the— He felt his stomach start to go as he thought of it, the shark or sharks, what had happened to Nonnie and Tsung. "Sharks—Jesus," he murmured.

Frost stood up, leaning hard against the edge of the upper bunk, realizing he was naked and clean. He rubbed his left hand, gingerly, across his face. The stubble was gone and his mustache felt trimmed.

He walked to the mirror in the bulkhead, unsteady still on his feet and stared at his face in the mirror there. He thought he detected more gray starting in his temples, but wasn't certain. He had one of the deepest tans he'd ever had, at least that he could recall. He took an unsteady step back. Someone had pulled him out of the water and he was aboard a private sailing ship or yacht. "The Deathwitch," Frost asked himself half aloud, almost shocked to hear the sound of his own voice.

A woman, though—the sheets, the perfume smell. A beautiful woman, he thought. It would go with the perfume smell. Perhaps some people yachting had seen him adrift. He studied his face in the mirror. His eyepatch was gone and he started to look for it, finding it near where he had slept. It looked as though it had been washed. He remembered more now— hearing shots when he'd seen sail two hundred yards behind him. Shots?

Someone aboard the vessel was a rifleman—a good one.

Frost found a closet—he didn't remember what they were called aboard a ship. He reasoned he needed something to wear. He opened the closet. There was plenty to wear, but nothing for him. Several shorts sets, two skirts, the kind that wrapped around and tied in the front, and an assortment of blouses. There was also a woman's robe. But in the corner, Frost saw what interested him. There was a rifle case.

Frost took the case out and set it on the floor, bending awkwardly because of his side. It was one of the suede Safariland cases, plush lined and with luggage handles. He'd seen them before, usually protecting expensive hunting rifles or—He unzipped the case full length. He recognized the gun—he'd seen them before. It was a Steyr-Mannlicher SSG with the green synthetic stock, possibly the most accurate production rifle in the world. It was a sniping rifle, rugged and reliable. Frost lifted it out of the case. The scope was a standard 3-9 variable Mannlicher model, with the Steyr mounts. The setting was at nine power.

He turned the rifle over in his hands, popping out the five-round rotary magazine.

He glanced at the spine of the magazine— transparent, he counted five rounds. Frost worked the bolt—the chamber was empty. He snapped the rear trigger, the bolt closed again, then barely touched the first trigger, the set so delicate the gun almost wished itself off.

"It's a 7.62mm," he heard the woman's voice say.

Frost started to move the muzzle of the rifle up, then remembered the magazine was out.

"Works better that way," she murmured.

Frost smiled.

"I mean, I assume you were interested in the rifle—either that or my dresses."

"There aren't any dresses," Frost smiled. "I looked already. You alone?"

"What—the closet?"

"Yeah," Frost smiled, starting to replace the rifle in the case.

"Should I tell you if I'm alone?"

"Unless there's another girl on board the same size, you're alone." He studied her face, the features soft but well defined, the cheekbones high and prominent, her skin tanned even more deeply than his. She had long hair, dark brown with a hint of red that he could see in the light streaming in behind her down the companionway steps. He couldn't tell quite how long her hair was because it was done up in a single, long braid, the braid half over her left shoulder, wisps of hair on her neck. She wore a two piece swimsuit and it left little for him to imagine about her, the dark blue of the suit seeming to heighten the tan of her skin. She took a step closer to him, Frost watching the rippling of the tiny muscles in her abdomen, the movement of her thighs. Her feet weren't naked—she wore sandals. There was a slender gold chain around her neck and as best he could tell at the distance, she wore no makeup.

"Do you want clothes—is that why you were—"

"I wanted to satisfy my curiosity," Frost answered, putting the rifle case back inside the closet and closing the door. "That's why I looked in the closet."

"It's a locker—not a closet. You're no seaman."

"You're right," Frost answered.

"Curiosity about what—me?"

"About who made a two hundred yard hit on a shark and with what?"

"I did and with that," she answered, her voice a soft, throaty alto.

"Wonderful."

"Do you want some clothes — I think you can get up on deck and get some air, then tell me about yourself."

Frost gestured toward the closet. "Not my style, kid."

"My brother keeps some swimming trunks and deck shoes around — probably find a shirt of his too. Look in that chest over there — unless you want me to do it. I don't know how you feel about nakedness."

"Yours or mine?" Frost asked.

"Yours — we can worry about mine later," and she turned and started up the companionway steps.

Frost looked after her. He looked after her longer than he felt he needed to and he looked after her still. "Beautiful," Frost whispered, half to himself, half to his surroundings.

Moving stiffly, he walked forward — he guessed it was forward — and found the chest to which the girl had referred. There were more of her things there and by lifting out the top of the chest — like a drawer — he found several men's things — swimming trunks and shorts and a pair of jeans and some shirts and deck shoes. The deck shoes were new. The size looked small, but he decided to give them a try. A pair of blue swim trunks and a dark blue shirt with a little reptile over the heart looked all right and he got into them.

The deck shoes were small, but fit and he closed the trunk, first replacing the drawer-like shelf. Frost started up the companionway steps, the sun low on the horizon behind him.

"Afternoon," he murmured to himself. Then he looked at the girl, almost directly beside him, leaning over the side, staring toward the sky. "What's your name?"

"Constanza," she smiled, turning to face him.

"Hank Frost," he told her. "You get some lead out of me?" and he pointed toward his side.

"9mms, I think—but I've done it before. My brother—one time it happened to him and he didn't want our uncle to know."

"Ohh," Frost nodded, looking forward, seeing the length of the ship. "You own this?"

"I guess I do—or maybe my uncle does—it doesn't matter—it's mine."

"Ohh," and Frost nodded.

"Your teeth had nicotine stains on them. I brushed them a little."

"Ohh," and Frost looked at the water, shrugging, not knowing what to say. "You always brush the teeth of strange men?"

"Sometimes," she smiled. "And I found a Zippo lighter in your shirt pocket. You had cigarettes? I couldn't find any."

"Yeah—guess I lost them," Frost shrugged.

"Here—I have plenty," and she handed him a box of Players Navy Cut. He popped open the box and took one, nodding as the girl lit it for him with a gold trimmed Dunhill lighter. "Hank Frost—it sounds like a strong name."

"Thanks," he smiled.

"Your friends were beyond—well, there was nothing I could do. You talked about them in your sleep, and about two women—that was all. One of the women you wanted to kill—you called her Eva—"

"Eva Chapmann," Frost added.

"The other woman you called Bess—I think you were making love to her in your delirium."

"Did I sound like I was good?" Frost smiled, not knowing what else to say.

"You have your eyepatch on again—I cleaned it for you."

"Thank you."

"You must tell me about it later, please?"

Frost only nodded, suddenly feeling tired and leaning against what seemed to be a chart desk. "Later," he whispered, coughing on the cigarette smoke. "Later."

"I don't think you have an infection," and he felt her cool hand on his forehead, then on his left cheek. "And you don't have a fever—just a little warm. A drink might do you good, but it might get you silly. All I was able to feed you was soup the last two days."

"A drink would be great," Frost nodded. "If I get silly, will you mind?"

"I don't think so," she smiled.

She disappeared below—funny, Frost thought, how nautical terminology like 'below' all came back to you. After a moment, she returned, a bottle of Myers dark rum in her right hand and two glasses in her left. "I have a friend who drinks this all the time," he smiled, taking the glass she offered and letting her fill it half way.

"He has good taste."

"O'Hara—naw—he just likes the stuff. Michael J. O'Hara doesn't have good taste in anything—and he'd be insulted if somebody thought he did."

"This O'Hara—a good friend?"

Frost thought about it a moment, then nodded, saying, "Yeah—maybe too good."

"What do you do, Hank Frost—what is a one-eyed man who knows little or nothing about the sea doing adrift in the middle of the Mediterranean?"

"Waiting for a pretty girl to pick him up," Frost smiled, the sweet rum burning his throat and his stomach and suddenly making him feel slightly light-headed.

"Was it worth the wait?" she smiled.

Frost nodded. "I think so, kid—I think so."

Chapter Ten

Frost looked at his watch. It was eleven—just after that, and it was dark in the cabin. Two drinks of the rum—he remembered when he tried sitting up and bumped his head again—had put him half out. He remembered the girl laughing as she'd helped him into the bunk or berth or whatever it was. He wasn't in the mood for nautical terminology now. She'd pulled off his shirt but left his trunks on.

Frost stood up, his head aching only a little now and found his shirt on the knob of the closet or locker or whatever it was. He pulled the shirt on over his head, calling out, "Constanza—where the—". He shrugged, getting his head through the hole and starting—wobbling—toward the companionway steps. His side still hurt, but not as badly as it had.

Topside, it was dark, the moon nowhere visible in the patchy cloud cover, but to the far north the sky was clear and he could see the brilliant patterns of stars against the blackness. Constanza was nowhere in sight. He started forward, holding to the railing as he crossed in front of what he mentally called the wheelhouse. He almost tripped over her, sitting on the deck beside the main mast. Again, Frost guessed—it seemed to be the largest mast.

She was smoking—he could tell from the smell on the comparatively cool night air that it was one of her Players.

"I was thinking," she said, looking up at him, her voice softer than he remembered it from earlier in the day.

"About what?"

"Do you remember making a pass at me?"

Frost thought a moment, then said, "I think I do."

"I decided."

"What did you decide?"

"I'll let you—into my pants, I mean."

"What a lovely way of putting it."

"When I was a little girl," she said, turning and looking out seaward, "some people killed my father and my mother, and tried to kill my brother and me. I remember my father always saying that he wanted us all to go on a vacation—I don't remember where. Anyway, I don't think he was ever very definite about it. But he wanted us to go—I remember that, and when my father and mother died, one of the things I thought about was that it was too late for the vacation. Do you know what I mean?"

She looked up at him and Frost only nodded, extending his hands to her, pulling her to her feet beside him. Her hair was loose now, the braid gone, the hair covering her bare shoulders and as she moved he could see she wore nothing but a skimpy pair of shorts, nothing on top, only the hair covering her breasts. There was a wind picking up and Frost didn't mind it as the wind caught her hair.

She looked down at her breasts, then up at his eyes.

64

"I'm too used to being alone out here."

"Is that why you have the rifle?"

"Yes—I suppose."

"Who are you—Constanza who?"

"Do you need to know?"

"No," Frost smiled, looking down at her. She was barefoot.

"Good—when you were drunk you told me you loved the woman Bess—does that mean you are faithful to her?"

"In my fashion," Frost smiled, adding, "isn't that in some song, I think?"

"I like songs—I like you too. I don't want to wait—that vacation thing. It might never come."

"All right," the one-eyed man whispered, the girl rising on her toes, her naked breasts against his chest. His right hand touched at the nipple of the left breast, for an instant only, but then her left hand took his and cupped his hand back over the nipple. "Do you want to go inside—or below decks or whatever the hell—"

"No—unless you need to. The deck, and your shirt under me—we could."

"What the hell—isn't my shirt anyway," he laughed; then he felt her lips touch his and he drew her close to him.

"Hank Frost," she murmured.

Frost didn't say anything. . . .

Chapter Eleven

The lines toward the east were a pale gray as Frost opened his eye, the girl still snuggled in his right arm. "It's beautiful, isn't it," he heard her whisper.

"One of my favorite lines from Shakespeare — never heard it quoted. It's from Julius Caesar, somewhere — 'Yon gray lines that fret the clouds are messengers of the day.' "

"You speak poetry," she smiled.

Frost traced a finger across her smile, saying, "Only sometimes — I'm not in a poetic business, kid."

"Heroic, then?"

"When guys like me are heroes, we're all in trouble," he smiled, bending over her quickly and kissing her slightly parted lips.

He felt her fingers touch at his neck, to hold his mouth down over hers. Her breasts were no longer naked, a blanket around her shoulders, half covering her during the night they'd spent on deck. As she moved closer to him now, the blanket slipped, past her shoulders, half down the length of her back as he bent to kiss at her neck. She moaned something he couldn't hear, the one-eyed man not thinking it was a word at any event.

He could feel her hands at his swimming trunks, pulling at the waistband, undoing the tie inside that kept them up around his waist. Frost freed his left hand and helped her with them, kicking the trunks away across the deck, leaning across her, her arms, still with the blanket covering them, folding around him.

Frost bent over her breasts, kissing first the left then the right, the coppery pinkish nipples coming erect under his touch. Her hands were on him, his penis coming hard under her fingers, the pressure of them maddening as he slipped down between her legs, her thighs wet feeling as he slid against them, almost punching his way inside her. There was a stiff breeze racing ahead of the sunrise now, and Frost could feel its coolness across his back, a contrast to the heat he felt where his skin touched hers.

His left hand was under her, at the small of her back, arching her up, feeling her abdomen pressing against his. She was biting at his neck, but gently, the pain almost heightening it, he realized. She sighed hard then, kissing at his ear, her body writhing under him, moving against him, around him, enveloping him.

As she started to almost sing softly to him, her body stiffening, Frost raised himself over her, both of them shuddering, together, sinking down, Frost's hands on her face, then his arms wrapping around her. The wind was stronger now, whipping at the blanket half covering them, catching her hair, making her skin seem to glow as Frost studied her eyes, the wildness there, the softness.

The blanket blew off in a gust of wind, catching

itself on one of the cleats.

Frost's eye turned down to stare at her, the perfection of her breasts, the symmetry of the subtle musculature of her abdomen and thighs, her arms stretched outward in rest as she smiled up at him.

Frost knotted the fingers of his left hand into the dark mane at the nape of her neck, pulling her face up to him, kissing her hard, tasting the saltiness of her mouth, feeling her tongue against his.

He pulled her head back, her neck arched, her throat exposed. He touched his lips to it, watching the fluttering of her eyelids, her eyes closed. Her lips moved and he bent his ear toward them to listen. She said, "I think I love you."

Frost kissed her lightly and folded his arms around her against the wind.

Chapter Twelve

It was one of the dresses from the trunk, white, soft looking and softer to his touch as his fingers brushed against it when he touched her shoulders. He waited beside her on the dock, wearing a pair of her brother's blue jeans, the same deck shoes and another one of the shirts with the little reptiles over the heart, this one dark blue as well.

The sun was strong, the wind calm except for momentary gusts blowing in off the harbor. Beyond the harbor, Frost could see the forbidding and barren rockscape of the island — Sicily. As the car drove along the wharf toward them and his hand over her hand felt her pulse quicken, he finally realized who and what the girl was. The car was a vintage Rolls Corniche Coupe, the top down and a driver and a second man in the front seat, both swarthy, clad in work clothes.

As the car stopped, the driver and the second man got out, both bowing slightly, one of them saying, "Donna Constanza." The second man — burly and with a prominent bulge under his shirt — opened the rear door. Frost let Constanza slide across, then stepped in, glancing down to the floorboards of the front passenger compartment — a shotgun. The barrels were short, very, and the side-by-side double with the rabbit ear hammers had a homemade leather sling attached to it. The gun was called a Lampara, Frost recalled. And he had seen them before, the weapon of the Sicilian Mafia bodyguard.

"Donna Constanza," Frost murmured to the girl. Her smile faded for an instant, then she drew closer to him and clutched his hands with both of hers. . . .

The house was a fortress, on a high rocky hill outcropping over a sparsely planted valley, terraced grape vineyards on the far side of the mountain that Frost had noticed as the Rolls, steaming hot with the open top, had traveled the gravel and rock strewn road.

The Rolls slowed at massive wrought iron gates and, the gates opened at the hands of a man almost identical to the driver and the bodyguard, a Lampara slung across his back.

The Rolls started up again, Frost eyeing the shotgun as the gates closed behind the car. A massive stone fountain dominated the central portion of the courtyard and ten or a dozen yards beyond it were low stone steps leading up into the small castle that was the home of the Donna Constanza — and Frost decided, the home of at the least the local Mafia chief, perhaps someone more important than that.

The Rolls stopped, a dust cloud puffing in the wake of the tire treads, the bodyguard, his Lampara now slung across his back, getting out and opening the door. Frost slid out and helped Constanza to the ground.

Almost instantly, he heard a woman's voice, old

sounding, the Italian guttural-sounding even to Frost's untutored ears, then as the one-eyed man turned, he saw the face belonging to the voice. An old woman, her head swathed in black scarves, and she was running, feebly, her arms widely outstretched.

Constanza sank against the woman's massive breast and held her, the woman kissing her, almost roughly touching at her cheeks and inspecting her suntan, touching at her hair.

Frost stood awkwardly, waiting. But suddenly the older woman bowed her head and moved away, the bodyguard and chauffeur doffing their hats.

Frost turned. Coming down the steps was a smallish man, neatly dressed in plain workers clothes—a rough looking blue shirt and wash pants, hunting or work boots on his feet. He wore a mustache, bristlingly waxed to tiny points at the outer reaches, his silvery grey hair slicked in place.

"Constanza—" Then the older man looked at Frost, saying, "I will speak in English, Signore—please come into my home." Constanza ran up the low steps, swept into the older man's arms, Frost hearing a word he recognized—zio, uncle.

Chapter Thirteen

Frost sat on the coolish veranda, watching the sunset, standing out of politeness suddenly as he saw Constanza entering from the library, feeling the breeze on his face now as he watched her, her uncle, Don Adolpho, walking more slowly behind her.

Constanza stood beside her chair, Frost holding it for her, but she didn't begin to sit, evidently, Frost thought, waiting for her vastly senior uncle to take his seat. Don Adolpho sat down, smiling benevolently to Constanza. She sat, Frost moving around to the other side of the table, then taking his own seat.

"I have made several telephone calls—your friend in New York—he gives you, ahh—" and he looked at Constanza, said something Frost didn't understand, then waited, Constanza speaking for him, "He gives you fine references, my uncle wishes to say."

Frost smiled, saying, "How is Joseph Canaretti—well, I hope?"

"Si—he is always well," and Don Adolpho lit a cigarette and gestured with it, as if dismissing the idea. "As is his daughter—I understand, you—ahh. Ha—we are both men of the world of course. My child thinks that I should help you."

Frost shrugged, glancing toward Constanza, then back at the Don, saying, "I'd be just as happy with a car to borrow or a telephone call—I need to contact some people and—"

"And ahh, what will these people, what will they do for you, heh?"

"Get me some money, another passport, a gun—some things like that."

"You need to recuperate—heh? This is true. And you are against an army, as I understand it, no? No?"

Frost shrugged, saying nothing.

"An army, heh? This, ahh—this Deathwitch—an evil name—"

"An evil lady," Frost interrupted.

"Si—but you must kill her before she kills you. And you say she already has all these other weapons."

"By now she's probably replaced whatever she lost aboard that freighter I told you about and her yacht. She's probably up and around. I must have opened up a bleeder when I shot her," Frost concluded. "But she's probably going all out to get her job done. She's like that."

"And her job—it is evil, si?"

"Yes," Frost nodded.

"I am what you might call a criminal—you know this?"

Frost nodded again.

"Constanza—she told me what happened to you, all of it, your Negro friend, the Chinese—how they died, what you tried to do. She wants that I help. But I am an old man and I did not reach old age by doing the whims of children. Her brother, I listened once to him and it cost him his life."

Frost watched Constanza's eyes, tightening—the way she had spoken, Frost had thought her brother was alive. "I do not do things for children's reasons," the Don went on. "But this is not a child's reason—this is a reason for men. I will help you to find this Deathwitch, what you do then will be your own affair. Agreed?"

It sounded like a question, but Frost knew that it wasn't. "Agreed," Frost said.

"Excellent—then you will stay with us while your wounds, they heal. My organization will find the trail of this Deathwitch for you, and some of my men will help you, at least for a time. Stay here, enjoy my home—but do not enjoy my niece more than she wishes," and the Don stood, and without waiting turned, and walked away.

Frost looked at the girl, almost whispering, "I thought you were practicing for a yacht race when you found me—but that death, it seems recent, of your brother."

"I was—practicing. But to kill myself," she said hoarsely. "My brother was," and she sighed heavily.

Frost stood up and walked to stop beside her, holding her hand, feeling her head sink against him.

"It was a year ago—my brother, Carlo, he wished to—I cannot tell you."

"I understand," Frost whispered.

"My mother and father—our mother and father—they were killed and my uncle killed their killers, killing them himself. When Carlo died, it was the first time in ten years my uncle has left the villa here—he found the man, then he took a knife and he—" She began to cry.

"I'm sorry," Frost told her, lamely.
"Hold me, Hank."
Frost nodded and held her.

Chapter Fourteen

Frost admitted to himself that he was having fun. With the guns the Don had collected over the years and what seemed like a limitless ammo supply for plinking, Frost felt akin to a kid in a candy store. He stood on the edge of a rocky promontory, two of the Lampara armed bodyguards in the distance, Constanza beside him, her Steyr in her hands, across a gorge a string of loose rocks at which Frost and the girl had been casually shooting for the last half hour. The range was a hundred yards and the girl and the rifle seemed mated to one another as she would shoulder it.

She shouldered the rifle again now, settling the scope on the rocky outcropping.

"You realize," she stated flatly, "why my uncle helps you — because I came back alive, with you. He thanks you for it and he chose to help you in order to repay this."

"I realize that," Frost answered, studying the Colt Gold Cup in his right fist.

"Do you like making love to me," she asked, Frost hearing the clicking of the rear set trigger as she settled the muzzle.

"I've done it enough these last few days," Frost told her. "Yes — I do."

"But there is still another woman."

"Yes."

"It doesn't bother me—I think."

"Good."

"Can you do this?" and she squeezed the first trigger, the rifle rocking against her shoulder, Frost's hands over his ears against the booming sound of the .308.

"With that rifle—I think so."

"No—with one of the pistols."

The rock she had evidently aimed for crumbled and turned to dust. "At a hundred yards," Frost asked, smiling.

"Yes—that Gold Cup, or any other pistol."

"I don't think so—but I can try."

Frost pushed the magazine release button, the seven round magazine dumping into his hand from the butt of the blued pistol. He checked the witness holes—he didn't like shooting guns he hadn't loaded himself. It belonged to the girl. Frost whacked the spine of the magazine against the palm of his left hand, seating the cartridges.

He stuffed the magazine in his belt—no more borrowed jeans from her dead brother, but clothes brought by the Don's personal tailor. Frost jacked back the Gold Cup's slide, flicking the slide stop up. He inserted the magazine up the butt of the pistol, giving it a firm pat on the base plate to seat it, then worked the slide release, the slide running forward, chambering one of the 185 grain jacketed hollow points. He upped the thumb safety, settling his fist around the flat back strap, his fingers curling around the checkered walnut grips.

"A hundred yards?" Frost tried to look and sound confident.

"Si," and as if to underscore her word, she worked the bolt on the Steyr, jacking out the spent case and chambering a fresh round.

"You've got ahh—you're taking advantage of me."

"Yes—but you do of me," she answered.

Frost looked at her, smiled, but said nothing.

"All right," and Frost settled the pistol in his hands, working down the thumb safety, feeling the grip safety submerge beneath the web of his right hand.

He picked a cluster of rocks, so that if he hit one, he could lie that he was aiming for that particular one all along. He lined up the Eliason rear sight with the front sight, steadying his breathing, edging his trigger finger against the trigger to get its feel.

Frost squeezed the trigger, the rock pile shifting, one of the rocks powdering, the .45 recoiling in his hands.

Frost upped the safety.

"A hot rock marksman—you'd call it that. Why was it important that I do that?" Frost smiled, marveling at his own luck. He had never made a one hundred yard first round hit with a handgun before in his life.

"I like a man to be better than me—at almost everything," she smiled, walking back toward the Corniche Coupe.

Frost rammed the pistol in his belt, the Lampara armed bodyguards watching him as he started after her. When he passed the nearer man, he rasped, "boogie-boogie."

He didn't get a laugh or a frown and decided he'd have to learn how to scare people in Italian.

Chapter Fifteen

Hank Frost had been told to dress for dinner, so now he stood in front of the full length mirror, checking his three piece white suit—one of the suits the Don had given him as a gift—and checking the knot of his black silk knit tie. He shrugged—somehow there were people who never cleaned up well. The shoes he wore now he imagined cost more than his usual sixty-five dollars. He didn't want to know how much more or he would have felt paranoid about scuffing them. He walked to the dresser top, seeing his new passport, leaving it there, seeing the FN High Power the Don had gotten for him and the half dozen spare magazines, and the new Gerber knife.

He took the pistol and weighed it in his hands, then set it down again and shrugged out of his jacket, going to the closet and getting the shoulder rig he'd been given with the pistol before trying it earlier that day.

He settled the shoulder rig—a European brand he didn't recognize—across his back and placed the High Power inside it, then tried the coat again. The full length mirror showed the outline of the gun.

Frost pulled off the coat, then the shoulder harness and threw the harness on the bed. He took the pistol and worked the slide, chambering the first round, then cautiously rolled down the hammer between the thumb and first two fingers of his right hand, working the trigger with his left hand.

He stuffed the pistol in his trouser band, butt forward, shrugging into the coat again. Nothing showed. . . .

Frost walked across the hallway and toward the dining room, the doors slid apart. The Don looked at him and smiled. "A pistol, my friend?"

"You said to dress for dinner," and Frost smiled, patting the gun under his coat. "You have a sharp eye, Don Adolpho."

"It is another reason why I am such an old man—si. Come, sit down, Hank."

Frost sat down, opposite Constanza, Frost and the girl flanking the Don.

"You have been to Morocco?"

"Yes," Frost answered the Don.

"I prefer business before dinner—it aids the digestion to have it out of the way. You will leave for there tomorrow, if that suits you. In Casablanca, there is a contact. And since Constanza insists on going with you, more than the two bodyguards I had originally planned to send will accompany you—there will be four. You must be very careful—I have enemies in Casablanca. I have always avoided the drug traffic—you know of this, I am sure. But there are persons in Casablanca who hate me for this. Besides the Deathwitch, you must be vigilant for them. All things beyond this will be explained in the morning. Now we eat," and the Don glanced past Frost and nodded.

"Vintage wine again—what a rut."

Chapter Sixteen

It didn't much resemble the movies, Frost thought, but driving through the high crime rate section of any town at midnight isn't the best way for a city to show off its fine points, he decided. Casablanca—named that because so many of the houses or 'casas' were originally white. He doubted that when the old Citroen reached its destination, the Club Panama, he'd find a grizzled black piano player or a lovely but tragic blonde. The one-eyed man shrugged his shoulders, turned to the man beside him—Demetrius—and started up a conversation.

"You always work for the Don?"

"Si—always."

"You've never worked for anyone else?"

"Si—never."

"Have you always been a bodyguard?"

"Si—always."

"You have never been interested in becoming, maybe an underboss to the Capo?"

"Si—never."

"Has your family worked for the Don's family?"

"Si—always."

"Never any other line of work?"

"Si—never."

"Are you always this talkative?"

"Si—always."

Frost shrugged his shoulders and looked out the window, at the closed tourist trap stands and markets, at the old section mud buildings, at the occasional man walking the darkened streets. Had he been on foot, the section would have given him the creeps, he thought, but with Demetrius beside him and one of the Don's other bodyguards, Alfonso, driving, Frost thought he had at least hedged the odds.

At the Club Panama they were to meet Achmed Munfi, a smuggler of grand scale and according to the diminutive Don's description, of grand proportions. Frost wondered if the man would wear a fez and sit in a Sidney Greenstreet fanback chair under a slowly whirling ceiling fan. Frost doubted it—he never had that kind of luck. But at least Achmed Munfi supposedly had information of the Deathwitch and her plans. And Munfi owed the Don, his smuggling operations out of Italy and into Italy under the Don's watchful eyes.

The Citroen stepped in a back alley, a bare bulb inside a mesh globe illuminating a green wooden door at the head of three low steps.

Frost stopped out of the Citroen, the driver Alfonso already out and holding the door for him. Frost felt for the FN High Power under the jacket of his light gray suit—the shape of the butt, the bulk, it was somehow reassuring under the circumstances.

Demetrius had a raincoat over his right arm. And under the raincoat, Frost knew Demetrius had a type of gun Frost would never consider trying—a twelve gauge double with the barrels sawn to ten inches and simply a heavy pistol grip, the grip weighted with lead to help hold it down against recoil. Alfonso was less dramatic. Bulging ever so slightly under his jacket, Frost could see the outline of what he knew was a Colt Python four-inch .357—one on each side.

Demetrius was the first to the door, Alfonso flanking Frost and slightly behind. As the door opened, under the glare of the bare bulb, Frost could see smoke drifting out—the smell was something he'd smelled in Viet Nam—hashish.

"Get high breathing around here," Frost remarked passing Demetrius and going inside first.

It was what he'd expected, yet hadn't really expected at all. The large man dominating the center of the room wore a fez, but no immaculate white suit, rather a sweat ringed pale blue shirt, his obesity imprinting on it in dark lines at his midsection.

Frost glanced over his shoulder to Alfonso, whispering, "I thought the Don didn't like drugs."

"The Don has discussed this many times with Signore Munfi—if Signore Munfi wishes to use drugs, that is his affair, but smuggling them in or out of Italy is something the Don will not permit."

"Sounds fair," Frost murmured.

Frost started across the room, more sweating bodies ringed in tiny groups around water pipes, Munfi himself sitting with three old men. "Club Panama floor show?" Frost smiled, extending his hand to Munfi.

"You are the American," the fat man belched. Frost could smell the hash on the man as he nodded.

"I have arranged for a mercenary soldier named

Kelsoe to meet with you behind the ramparts past the Casbah, near where the coastal littoral and the sea join."

"What?" Frost looked at the man.

"The coastal littoral—the seacoast, near the harbor."

"There really is a Casbah?"

"Of course," the fat man nodded.

"When?" Frost asked, watching the nervous looks in Alfonso's and Demetrius's eyes.

"At one-o'clock—you have just the time to get there—our roads are very good—my best wishes and felicitations to the Don."

"Thanks," Frost nodded, turning and starting to go.

"Ohh—Captain Frost—"

Frost turned and looked back at the fat man. "Yes?"

"You are to go alone—otherwise, Mr. Kelsoe might not wish to come out."

"You got a line into Kelsoe?"

"Yes? A line?"

"Can you reach him between now and then?"

"Yes," the fat man said, as though saying something of vast importance.

Frost decided that perhaps it was that important. "Ask him to make sure he's there—or otherwise, if he doesn't meet with me, I'll find him. And he probably wouldn't like that," Frost stated flatly. "I never make threats—and you can tell him that too, but this is more important to me than he might think. So it isn't a threat or anything—just the plain truth. Now you tell him that."

As Frost started through the door out of the Club Panama, he tried remembering which western movie he'd heard that in.

Chapter Seventeen

There was a bright moon and Frost stared up at it a moment, then toward the ground along the narrow sliver of land separating the walls of the old city and the waters óf Casablanca harbor. There was no sign of Kelsoe, the mercenary of whom Munfi had spoken. Frost checked the black luminous face of the Rolex Sea-Dweller on his left wrist. It was one o'clock, time for the meeting.

Frost looked behind him, at Alfonso and Demetrius, saying, "He wanted this to be alone, so let's make it that way—take the car and drive off up there past the walls and wait for me."

"It is a trap for you, Signore Frost," Alfonso said definitively.

"I know that—but I've got to get information on Eva Chapmann, so trap or not, I've gotta go. Let them spring it. You hear any shots, come running, huh?"

"Si," Demetrius nodded.

Alfonso didn't nod—he was already starting back toward the Citroen.

Frost reached under his coat, buttoning out the magazine in the Browning and cupping his hand over the ejection port to catch the chambered round. He locked back the slide, re-magazined the first round and gave the magazine a whack, seating the cartridges, then reinserted it. He released the slide stop, letting the slide run forward on its rails. The hammer still at full stand, he upped the thumb safety and replaced the pistol in his belt, but toward the front of his waistband now, less comfortable and concealable, but faster and more accessible.

Opening his necktie to half mast, he started up the sandy causeway between the city walls and the harbor waters. The whiteness of the sand, the bleached whiteness of the old city walls under the moonlight made his way clear. Still, he could see no one.

The one-eyed man stopped, hearing something to his right as he walked beside the wall. He decided there was someone on the wall. His palms sweating, he kept walking, his right hand edging across his abdomen slightly, to get nearer to his pistol.

He could hear a low, rumbling sound in the water to his left as he ascended the walkway along the wall.

There was no Kelsoe and whether the fat old smuggler who smoked hash knew it or not, it was a trap. Frost kept walking, waiting for the right second to move. There was no cover, nothing but the wall itself and it was too smooth to even provide a large enough niche in which to hide. If attackers would come from the sea, he would be caught in a crossfire.

His mind raced. They would expect him to move, at any time now, to race ahead toward shelter at the far end of the wall, nearer to him now than the opposite end of the wall from which he had come.

He could hear the almost living throb of the launch

engine, perhaps more than one—he didn't look around.

The one-eyed man nodded to himself, trying to feel for the right second to move. If they fired ahead of him, then running back could buy him seconds. He needed that, and the closer to the end of the wall from which he had come, the greater chance that Alfonso and Demetrius would link up with him, that their fire support would do some good.

Mentally, he tried gauging what good a sawed-off double, two Colt Pythons and a High Power would do against submachineguns, perhaps worse. He swallowed hard, stopping, snatching a Camel from his outside coat pocket, then lighting it—his hands trembling slightly—in the blue-yellow flame of his battered Zippo.

He dropped the lighter in his pocket, standing there for a few seconds, inhaling the smoke deep into his lungs, exhaling it hard through his nostrils, almost listening to his heart pound inside of him.

Frost inhaled again on the cigarette, then spit it from his lips, grabbing at the High Power as he wheeled and started to run. It was easier going down hill—he had the thought just as the power boat now off to his right as he retraced his steps, started to open fire, the wall behind him chipping, fragments pummelling him, sand under his feet kicking up under the impact of the submachinegun fire.

There was a second boat, speeding in from further out in the harbor, more subgunners aboard it, opening fire, despite the too-great distance. From the wall above him, Frost hear the rattle of automatic rifle fire.

Frost, his arms extended at his sides, his head held back and mouth open to gulp air, bent his body into a dead run.

The High Power in his right fist barked twice, toward the nearer power boat, and as Frost glanced toward it, he could see the inky black water rippling where his bullets had impacted.

He kept running, the submachinegun fire getting closer. He dove for the sand, the wall beside which he had run pulverized under the impact of the gunfire.

He heard a loud booming sound, then another— heavy pistol shots. Looking up as he snapped off two shots and started to his feet again, he could see Alfonso, one Python in each hand, running toward the end of the wall, close at his heels Demetrius, the little sawed off shotgun in both his fists, the raincoat that had covered it gone.

Frost started to run again, glancing up toward the wall, hitting the sand as the automatic rifle there opened up again. He rolled onto his back, the sand on both sides of him spraying up under the impact of the rifle slugs. He pumped the High Power's trigger twice, then twice again, brushing sand from his face as he started to his feet, the rifleman from the top of the wall careening over the side.

Frost kept running, hearing the revving of the power boat engine nearest him. There were more of the booming pistol shots and as Frost glanced to his right, he could see one of the subgunners aboard the nearer launch toppling over the side of the launch and into the water, his gun still chattering as he fell.

Frost was within fifty yards of the edge of the wall now, Alfonso firing his pistols, one in each hand.

Forty yards and the subgun fire from the farthest launch was coming up on him, starting to strafe the wall.

Frost hit the sand again, firing the High Power toward the farthest launch, nailing the driver or boatman—Frost couldn't be certain what to call him, but the windshield cracked and the boat suddenly veered off hard to Frost's right

Frost was on his feet again, running. Thirty yards.

"Signore!"

It was Demetrius, running toward him, Alfonso by the edge of the wall, firing his pistols, the .357 mags bright flashes in the semi-darkness, orange tongues leaping outward as the revolvers boomed.

"Signore!"

The nearer launch was coming ashore, two men already piling out of it, submachineguns firing as Frost hit the sand again, rolling, firing at them, nailing the nearest man as Frost spent out his magazine.

The High Power's slide locked back and Frost dumped the magazine, fumbling a spare as the second subgunner fired toward him.

"Signore!"

Frost hear a loud blast, like a tiny bomb going off.

The subgunner wheeled, firing toward the sound and Frost glanced to his left. Demetrius, ten yards away, stood his ground, firing the little sawed-off's second barrel. There was a loud, almost animal-like scream and the subgunner went down, his gun still firing.

"Signore!"

Frost looked toward Demetrius—the man was

down, writhing in the sand.

Demetrius' white suit pants were stained dark in the legs. The man screamed. Frost, the new magazine in place, worked the slide stop and as soon as the slide locked into battery, the one-eyed man fired, two rounds into the head of the wounded subgunner in the sand, then the pistol locked in both his fists, he fired twice more at the last remaining man in the nearer launch.

He couldn't see the hits, but he could see the body snap backward and fall.

Firing his pistol, Frost started across the sand, hearing the booming of Alfonso's Pythons behind him. Frost stooped to the dead subgunner, snatching up the weapon—an Uzi. From the man's trouser band, he grabbed three fresh magazines, dumping the partially spent magazines already in place and loading the fresh one.

Advancing across the sand, he opened fire with the Uzi, the High Power in his belt.

The second launch was fifty yards off, the subgunner firing. Frost fired toward them, the sand near his feet chewing up as he started into the surf. He dropped the Uzi's spent magazine into the water, loading a fresh one in place, then scrambled over the gunwales into the drifting powerboat.

The second launch's gunners were quiet for an instant.

Frost set down his Uzi, grabbing the dead man still in the launch by the lapels of his plaid sportscoat, pulling him, pushing him over into the water and spitting after him.

Frost lit a cigarette, holding the butt in the left

corner of his mouth as he tested the powerboat's throttle.

There was a rumbling sound, a gurgling, the engine suddenly seeming to roar as Frost stood behind the wheel. He threw into reverse, backing the boat away from the sand, tossing his cigarette into the water. He cut back into a forward speed—he wasn't sure which, but the engine responded.

He started to accelerate, taking the launch out toward the farther boat. The boat was turned out to sea now and the subgunners aboard her were firing.

Frost reached behind him, snatching at the Uzi, slinging it under his right arm and letting out the controls of the powerboat. "Whiplash," he laughed, feeling his neck snap back slightly as the boat lurched across the incoming breakers, in pursuit of the farther launch.

Frost wondered if it were that his boat was inherently faster, or that he was more reckless out of ignorance of watercraft generally. He was gaining on them.

He glanced up at the moon, almost squinting against its brightness now, the wind lashing at his hair, his face and his clothes sodden from the spray as he stood behind the controls. His Uzi rested now across the frame of the bullet-shattered windshield, the safety off, his finger just outside the trigger guard.

One of the subgunners aboard the launch ahead of him—now less than thirty yards, was apparently out of ammo. He was shaking the gun, violently. Frost watched him in the bright moonlight. The second subgunner was still firing, but then too, his subgun stopped.

Frost let out the controls all the way, the powerboat under him lurching forward as the tachometer nearly redlined, his right fist tightening on the Uzi. One of the subgunners had a pistol in his hands, firing, the glass near Frost shattering still more, bullets pinging off the hull of the powerboat.

Frost kept his boat going, full throttle. The distance was less than twenty yards now and both of the subgunners had pistols firing. Frost turned the wheel, cutting a wide wake through the water, hard port, to pass the craft, to circle it, keeping up his speed, running his wake around it, the second powerboat starting to swamp.

The men aboard were still firing, Frost hearing the bullets pinging off his hull, off the seat back in front of which he stood.

Locking his left fist on the steering wheel, to keep the momentum of the arc, Frost pressed the Uzi tightly against him resting the stubby muzzle on the windshield frame, his trigger finger twitching. A three round burst tore through the windshield of the enemy boat, the man behind it spinning, twisting and falling over the gunwales.

Frost fired again, toward one of the two remaining men, now huddled in the gunwales of the runaway boat. A three round burst, then another, then another and one of the men fell backwards, hands to his face. Frost thought he heard a scream, but told himself it was imagination—the roar of the powerboat's engine was too loud, the thrashing of the waves around it too much noise to hear something like a scream.

One man was left.

Frost wanted him alive. He set the Uzi down, the safety on, cutting his wheel sharp, starting to aim the bow of his boat toward the second boat, the boat spinning in the wake of Frost's craft.

Then yards, five, four—Frost cut the wheel hard port and took a running leap, hurtling his body across the narrow gap of water between the two craft, landing hard, skidding across the engine cowling of the second boat.

Before he could move, he felt the man on him, clawing at his face and throat. Frost rammed his elbow back, into the man's face, hearing the squeal and scream of the man's pain.

Frost was on his knees, pulling the man up from the deck, his hands on the man's throat and ear. Frost hauled his right fist back, hammering it forward across the already bloody pulp of face, hammering the man back against the pilot's seat.

Frost was on his feet now, reaching down with his left, grabbing a handful of greasy hair, dragging the half unconscious man to his feet.

"Where is she—Eva Chapmann?"

Frost could hear his own voice as if it belonged to someone else—he had never heard such anger there.

The High Power was in his right fist. The man shouted at him, blood spurting from his mouth, lisping as he spoke. "I don't—she hired—a man in Tangier called—don't know the name—he called us to kill an American—I know—"

Frost shoved the man back against the engine cowling, reaching to the controls. He could feel it in the hairs on the back of his neck; wheeling, the High Power snaking forward as the man raised a boat hook to crash it down into Frost's head. Frost fired his pistol twice, the muzzle inches from the man's face.

The head exploded.

Chapter Eighteen

Demetrius, a shot of morphine for each leg, was moaning in his semi-conscious delirium, in the back seat of the Citroen.

Alfonso parked and Frost climbed out.

"You wanna wait with him," Frost asked.

"Demetrius will lose his legs?"

"I think so—if that's all he loses," Frost said frankly.

"I will go inside—the old fat one—he made the trap. I will kill him."

"All right," Frost nodded, suddenly respecting Alfonso and the wounded Demetrius more than he had. Gangsters, gunmen—but men. Frost had the High Power in his belt, a liberated Uzi under his water- and blood-stained jacket as he turned the knob on the back door into the Club Panama.

This time the door was locked.

Frost swung the Uzi forward and whipped off the safety, running a five round burst into the locking mechanism of the door as he stepped back, then kicking it in with his right foot. He started through the doorway. The fat man with the fez—Munfi—was into his hashish, but this time rather than writhing bodies surrounding him there were a half dozen men — his bodyguards.

Frost opened fire as the nearest man went for the riot shotgun.

He could hear the booming behind him of the twin .357s Alfonso carried. Frost sprayed the Uzi toward two more of the bodyguards, the men going down as they opened fire. Alfonso nailed another man with his pistols, the body flying back, half across the lap of the fat man with the fez. The fat man was screaming.

Frost stopped his subgun, letting it hang at his side as Alfonso walked toward the fat man.

Alfonso muttered something guttural-sounding in Italian that Frost couldn't understand — the fat man didn't understand it either.

Frost wondered if he would have understood his own name. Both pistols were leveled at his face. Frost turned his head away as the guns roared. "Good-bye," the one-eyed man murmured.

Chapter Nineteen

The roadway between Tangier and Casablanca was good but dusty and hot. Frost tried to sleep, but kept awakening, remembering what had happened to Demetrius' legs after they'd found a doctor that could be trusted. The legs had been cut off.

The thought made Frost want to vomit—it could have been him, his legs. He thought back to when he had lost his eye, awakening from surgery with both eyes bandaged, the nurses, the doctors—no one wanting to say just exactly what had happened.

Finally, he'd ripped the bandages away and half drunk with the drugs they'd put in him, stumbled, bleeding, toward the mirror. He'd seen the gaping hole and screamed, collapsing from the exertion and the loss of blood.

But Demetrius wouldn't be able to stumble anywhere, to walk ever again. Sometime after he came out of the drugs, he'd realize there was nothing beneath his crotch in the bed, that his legs were gone.

Alfonso had left the younger man his sawed off shotgun, loaded—to give him the option of not living with the loss.

Staring out at the desert dawn, Frost wondered if

Demetrius would exercise the option or not, and the thought sickened and saddened him. . . .

Frost stood under the steaming hot water, the water streaming down his hair and across his body. He had slept only fitfully throughout the long ride across the mountains and the desert, been nervous throughout the stops made for gasoline and for food and water. The hotel in Tangier had been a welcome relief, but there had been no real sleep for him. The old Don had personally spoken with him on the phone. Constanza had been brought back to Sicily, against her wishes, but for her safety. Demetrius had apparently elected not to die. The old Don somehow sounded proud of that, like a father speaking of one of his children, vowing Demetrius would be cared for and that Frost had all of the Don's resources at his command in his hunt for the Deathwitch—to avenge Demetrius.

There had been more calls to learn the whereabouts of the other fat man who wore a fez whom Frost knew of—but this one a man to be trusted, Mahmed. Working for the Greek arms merchant, Nikos Kalantos, he had aided Frost and Julie Pulman* in acquiring the arms necessary for their assault on the sheikdom of Sheik Ali Hassan Foudani and afterward, aided Frost and the rescued woman for whom Julie Pulman had jeopardized her life. Frost thought of the lovely, almost exquisite Julie Pulman and her fate. The idea didn't calm him.

Frost turned off the water and stepped out from

* See They Call Me The Mercenary #7, *Slave of the Warmonger*

behind the glass doors, toweling himself dry and studying his face in the mirror. Over the years, the scar from his missing eye had healed and it was no longer so sickening, as it had been that first time years earlier.

He took a fresh black patch and secured it in place covering where his eye had been, noticing the fine line of lighter skin the ties for the patch made where the sun didn't strike his face.

He shook his head, starting into the bedroom of the small suite. He glanced at the Rolex on his left wrist, smudged away a droplet of water and read the time. He had ten minutes before his meeting in the lobby with a representative of Mahmed who would have the details of their meeting. Mahmed was being careful these days, Frost understood. With all the terrorists, the backwater self-styled governments and all, being an arms dealer could be a hazardous profession, for even just the African representative for an arms dealer as Mahmed was for Kalantos.

Frost shuffled through his Safariland SWAT bag, finding matching socks and a pair of underpants, then shucked into his white suit, leaving the vest because it was too hot. He knotted an Italian silk black knitted tie around his neck, leaving it at half mast, then stuffed his pockets with money, identification, spare magazines for the High Power and his room key. He checked the High Power for a loaded chamber and full magazine, then stuffed it inside his trouser band, butt forward behind his left hip. He clipped the tiny Gerber MkI Boot Knife into place on his right side inside his pants.

As he started out the door, he remembered he was

to be reading the newspaper when Mahmed's men would make contact with him in the lobby. He picked up the folded copy of Al-Anba, the official Moroccan government newspaper and studied it. He couldn't read it. He shrugged and took it anyway.

He avoided the elevator to the lobby, taking the stairs instead. He stood for a moment, half way down the last flight, taking in the lobby. He saw no one remarkable, but he removed the newspaper from his jacket pocket and glanced at it, obviously, then started down the remaining treads to the lobby floor.

There was an overstuffed chair vacant beside a potted palm, near enough under a ceiling fan to feel it stirring the air. But that was illusion, Frost realized. Like his small suite, the lobby was air conditioned. The fan was only trim.

The one-eyed man sank into the overstuffed chair and began looking at the newspaper in earnest. He glanced down at his watch once, trying to puzzle out a caption under an interesting looking photo. He was just about to give up, hearing his name called.

He looked up. The man was thin, weasely looking, like a character out of an old movie, a white suit, more rumpled than Frost's, hung like a sack from his shoulders and waist. "Captain Frost?" the man repeated.

"Yes," Frost nodded.

"You are interested in the whereabouts of—"

"Mahmed," Frost smiled.

"Mahmed asked that you recount to me the death of Julie Pulman."

Frost felt the corner of his mouth turn down. "Her tongue was cut out by Ali Hassan Foudani and after I rescued her, she took her own life with a gun."

"You are Captain Frost indeed. Mahmed wishes to meet with you at the museum that was once the sultan's palace in Medinah, the old town. In twenty mintues. Our roads are excellent, and this rendezvous should be easily met."

"Yes," Frost nodded. "Any taxi driver can find it?"

"Yes—or I can take you there myself."

"Fine," Frost nodded. He stood up, looking at the man, vastly shorter than himself. "There is a friend I must not miss—he's in his room. I'll leave a message I'll be gone."

Without waiting for a reply, Frost started toward the front desk. He didn't like museums—you always had to be careful for metal detectors and fluoroscopic devices that could spot a gun.

Chapter Twenty

He'd read the guidebook. Part of the original fifteenth century ramparts still enclosed the old city, and beyond these in the city built by the French all avenues began at Muhammed the Fifth Square. They were entering the medinah now, like a different world from Frost's hotel near United Nations Square in the business section. The temperature was in the low seventies and there was a breeze, some of it penetrating the back seat through the wide open windows of the Fiat in which Frost rode.

From the wide avenues of the French city, the warren of narrow streets in the old town seemed alien, almost forbidding to him. He glanced through the windows at the stone houses and at the people who walked the narrow streets who sometimes glanced back at him.

"The European quarters are all either south or west of here, captain," the man called over the front seat back. "But since our independence, the European population has progressively declined."

"Sorry to hear that," Frost smiled, not knowing what else to say.

"We are not going to the museum—that was a ruse

in the event you decided to leave word to a colleague," the man called.

Frost had his right fist on the High Power, the muzzle low but pointed through the seat back. "Where are we going then."

"Mahmed wishes to meet you nearby, at the Great Mosque, on the steps there."

"Why the switch—just so no one—"

"There was no distrust of yourself implied, Captain Frost. But Mahmed is very wary these days. These are perilous times."

Frost smiled, thinking he'd heard that line before. "All right," and he returned the High Power to his trouser band, but left it cocked and locked.

The Fiat stopped after a few minutes before a vast structure, Frost getting out, standing beside the battered car for a moment studying the Great Mosque. There was something about Moslem religious architecture, at once aesthetically stunning yet warm.

"I can't go inside, can I?"

"It would not be advisable," the driver warned.

"You gonna wait?"

"Mahmed has transportation available for you both."

"Wonderful," and Frost started to dig in his pockets for cash, but the Fiat was already starting away.

He shrugged and checked his watch. Almost precisely twenty minutes had passed since first meeting the mysterious little man in the lobby. Mahmed was a business person and would be prompt, so Frost started toward the steps, dodging a small Japanese truck driving too fast, crossing the street and studying the structure as he approached it.

A car pulled alongside the curb, a Mercedes and the rear door swung open, Frost's hand reaching for his gun.

"Captain Frost—please, there is no need."

Frost stooped down to peer inside the back seat. A bright red fez, a white suit draping a massive body—it was his friend Mahmed. "My friend—thank you for coming," the one-eyed man smiled.

"Please—we will talk soon. Join me."

Frost looked over his shoulder once, then stepped inside the car, slamming the door behind him.

"Ali—my home," Mahmed said to the driver. Frost looked across the seat as the Mercedes pulled away from the curb, blending into the traffic. "You have great troubles—but so do I. All from this woman they call by the ludicrous name the Deathwitch."

"Not too ludicrous, really," Frost remarked, lighting a Camel. "She feeds on death and if ever a woman were a witch, it's Eva."

Mahmed nodded soberly, murmuring, "Perhaps then, not ludicrous at all."

He smiled then and pressed a button on the seat arm beside him, a small bar unfolding from the front seatback. "My troubles and yours have made me momentarily forget my manners. If I recall correctly, your drinking tastes are varied."

Frost nodded, eyeing the bottle of scotch. "As long as it's free."

Chapter Twenty-One

"So, we were on the boat and the sharks were attacking and the boat started to seven and one-half," Frost told Mahmed.

"Seven and one-half?"

"Capsize—capsize? Get it? That's my capsize and that's what the boat—never mind," and Frost poured himself another glass of scotch.

"Things have not gone well for you since we last have seen one another. I have heard things in passing from friends."

"You're right," Frost whispered, setting down his drink, only half finished. He rubbed his hands across his face, feeling the eyepatch as he did. "Things have not gone right," he sighed heavily.

"And you come to me—I am honored. I think our mutual problem is not all that troubles you though," Mahmed remarked.

Frost leaned back in the overstuffed chair, away from the low table. Momentarily, he studied Mahmed's house. Oriental rugs covered the floors and hung like pictures from the long wall opposite him beyond the low steps leading into the living quarters of the house. Brass bowls and pitchers were on tiny shelves along the near wall to Frost's left, a ceiling fan swirling lazily above their heads. Mahmed filled, almost to overflowing, a rattan fan back chair, holding his fruit juice in his stubby fingers, waiting silently for Frost to speak.

"You are troubled," Mahmed finally said as Frost lit a cigarette.

"Yeah," the one-eyed man nodded. "My life I think—that troubles me. The woman I love—her name is Bess. I wonder—I wonder if, hell—I don't know," and Frost shook his head.

"You wonder if your life can change for her?"

"Yes," Frost answered, the warmth and the mellow feeling of the scotch dissipating rapidly.

"She loves you greatly?"

"Yes," Frost answered.

"And by your own words you love her equally well, so a question then."

Frost looked at the fat Arab and nodded. "A question then—what?"

"If she were to change the color of her hair, as women sometimes do, would you love her less or more?"

"Of course not."

"But if she were to change the way she thought, the way she expressed her beliefs, the very beliefs themselves, would this change your relationship?"

"I don't—I don't know. It might, because then she'd be a different person, wouldn't she?"

"Then you have solved your own problem, my friend. If the woman is in love with you, then that is indeed whom she loves. Were you to cease being Hank Frost, then you might well cease being the object of her love. It is a failing of western relationships. Two persons will be in love, and one tries to change the other and eventually succeeds, or one of the lovers will endeavor to change himself. And changed, now, they wonder why they no longer love. But they are different people, having forced this difference to come about. We change, all of us, naturally, and man and woman can grow and change together and this natural change is good. But when the change is unnatural, is forced—the person can sometimes be lost."

"You used to teach philosophy, right," Frost smiled, lighting another cigarette.

"I have never taught philosophy, but I have studied it greatly. Not from books, but from the people I have known. If this woman loves you, then you are whom she loves, and were you to change for her,—has she asked that you do this?"

"No."

"What makes you then, think that you should?" Mahmed asked.

"Well—hell, you know that—what I do, what I am—"

"But what you are is what she loves, and if this is not so, why doesn't she love another instead of you?"

"She, ahh—I don't know," Frost shrugged, feeling intellectually outclassed.

"Precisely—but she does. She knows, as you know of her."

"You charge for house calls?" Frost smiled.

The Moslem laughed, saying nothing.

"Before my long range problems can test your theory, we still have that other matter, don't we?"

"Eva Chapmann," Mahmed sighed. "What a

distressing woman. The direct opposite, I should say, of your woman Bess."

"Yes," Frost agreed.

"She attempted to secure the services of myself in her endeavors—I refused. She then attempted to make contact directly with Mr. Kalantos. He refused her, as I knew he would. Mr. Kalantos, as do I, has professional ethics. To sell arms to anyone named Chapmann, whether her late father, or Eva Chapmann herself, would be evil. "And this woman's objectives were obvious to me from the start—she presented letters of credit and I at once recognized the source. Were she to be successful, she might well precipitate the next World War."

"World War III?"

"Westerners count wars like points in a baseball competition. In the east, there are wars too numerous to count. But yes, what you label a third World War."

"Who was she buying for?" Frost asked.

"A most curious person indeed—I believe the English word is anachronism, to mean out of synchronization with time?"

"Yes—anachronism."

"Her client or employer, however you chose to phrase the relationship, is this—an anachronism."

Frost smiled, thinking Mahmed seemed pleased with the word. Then Frost's overstuffed chair exploded at the back, where his head had been before he leaned forward to lift up his drink. And Mahmed, his eyes wide open, tumbled forward from his chair, the chair back splintered and the fat man's white suit coat splotched with blood.

The bright red fez rolled across the Oriental rug.

Chapter Twenty-Two

Frost rolled out of his chair, the FN High Power coming into his right fist, this thumb swiping at the smallish safety. There were more shots, the glass doors leading into the patio completely disintegrating as three men dressed in Arab clothes, Uzi submachine-guns in their hands, burst through into the sitting room.

Frost pumped the High Power's trigger twice, two shots impacting into the stomach of the nearest man, the man's body spilling forward, half across Mahmed, less than a yard from Frost's feet.

The one-eyed man reached across the open expanse of Oriental rug and snatched at the Uzi, rolling left then as the chair beside him took a burst of automatic weapons fire.

Frost had the Uzi in his hands now, in a firing position, rolling onto his back from behind the shelter of a massive writing desk, pumping a three round burst toward the two men by the shattered doors.

One of the two men went down, the second man firing, the desk beside Frost splintering under the impact of the full metal case subgun ammo.

Frost fired the Uzi again, missing, an answering

subgun burst tearing into the wall behind him. Frost tucked back closer to the wall, behind the shelter of the desk.

He could hear the sounds of running feet in the courtyard, during a lull in the subgun fire.

Frost fired another burst, the subgun going dry after the third shot. There was a long answering burst from the man by the doors, then the distinct absence of gunfire in the middle of the string as the subgunner's Uzi went dry. Frost rolled from behind the desk, the High Power in his left fist.

He could see it, almost as if it were slow motion, the man beside the door struggling a fresh stick into his Uzi, the startled look in the eyes half shrouded like the face behind the folds of a burnoose. Frost pumped the trigger of the High Power, twice, then twice again, the subgunner's body starting to spin, the full magazine in the Uzi, the subgun firing upward into the ceiling as the man stumbled, fell and went flat on the rug in the broken glass.

Frost started to his feet, half stumbling across the room, grabbing up the second dead man's Uzi and snatching two spare magazines from the man's sash.

He dropped to his knees, firing the Uzi as three more men started through the frames of the glass doors, Uzis firing in their hands. Frost fired the liberated subgun, hosing it across the space the three men filled, one going down, another crumpling to his knees, wounded but still firing, the third backing off behind the door frame.

Frost's right shoulder felt the ripping and tearing and he lurched to his left, the Uzi falling from his fingers. But the High Power was still in his belt as the second man stumbled to his feet and started to fire again. Frost had the pistol in his left fist, his thumb awkwardly twisting behind the backstrap of the grip to work down the safety. He started to fire, too soon, his hand not fully in position, the slide biting deep into the web, the spur of the hammer pinching into the backside of the venus mound between his thumb and first finger. But the subgunner went down.

His left hand bleeding all over his pants, Frost took the pistol in his right fist, the pain when he moved his right arm intense.

He pushed himself to his feet, waiting for the third man behind the door frame.

The man started out, firing and Frost fired his High Power once, then once again, then hurtled himself to the floor behind the ripped apart overstuffed chair.

He could hear the rattle of the subgun, hear the shattering sounds as glass and plates around the room smashed. Then there was nothing.

Frost, his left hand bleeding badly, his right arm throbbing and the sleeve of his jacket already soaked red with blood, pushed himself to his knees, extending the muzzle of the High Power past the chair back, then peering around from behind it. Six dead men lay on the floor, a small fire burning in the near corner where stray gunfire had apparently caused an oil lamp to shatter.

The fire was spreading now, Frost pushing himself to his feet. He rolled one of the bodies off Mahmed, feeling for a pulse with the back of his bleeding left hand. Mahmed was alive. Frost rolled him over, but only enough to see if Mahmed's air passages were clear.

The sweating eyelids fluttered open, Mahmed coughing up blood, whispering hoarsely, "Reginald Field—the house of Reginald Field, beyond the city on the old road from the Great Mosque—white house, white Rolls Royce in the drive—doctor there—doctor there—" Mahmed's eyes closed, the breathing labored sounding.

Frost rocked back on his haunches wondering if it were physically possible for him to move the massive Arab, his friend.

He started to try, wondering about the name Mahmed had used. He knew it, probably half the people in the English speaking world knew it. Reginald Field. Physician turned mystery novelist, consistently topping the best seller lists. Frost had just read Field's latest book when he was in the London hospital. As he started trying to shoulder Mahmed, he felt sorry for himself. If he'd brought the book along, he could have had it autographed.

Chapter Twenty-Three

Frost parked the Mercedes — the chauffeur had been murdered, his throat slit — in front of the massive wrought iron gates to the white house. He could see the Rolls Royce, not in the drive, but parked inside an open garage, the moonlight bright enough that Frost had been able to see the house sufficiently clearly from the road.

Frost glanced onto the back seat, Mahmed stretched cumbersomely across it on his chest, the gunshot wounds in his back and shoulder packed with towels Frost had taken from the Arab's house.

He could have scaled the wrought iron gates, easily, but not with Mahmed, and Reginald Field was apparently a close friend to the Arab. Frost climbed out of the car and started toward the gates on foot, gravel crunching under his feet.

There was a television monitor on the gate and a microphone and a push to call switch. Frost pushed the switch, once, then once again. He glanced to the Rolex on his wrist, watching the second hand sweep once around the black luminous dial, then once more. He started to push the call button again, but there was a humming sound and a crackle from the microphone/speaker. "Yes—what do you want?"

It was a woman's voice, throaty, good-sounding despite the distortion of the microphone/speaker.

"My name is Hank Frost—I'm a friend of your friend Mahmed—the fat man with the fez. He's been injured pretty badly—said your husband or whoever, could help—Reginald Field."

"Reginald Field isn't my husband. But I know Mahmed. What happened—and what happened to you?"

Frost glanced into the television camera, then at his bloodstained right arm. "We were both injured at the same time. Can we come in?"

"Give me a moment to pull something on—yes. Start up the driveway. I'll meet you at the door."

Frost glanced back toward the Mercedes. "You might get Reginald Field to come out and give us a hand, or a male servant or whatever. Mahmed can't walk and my arm—it's hard to—"

"I understand." The speaker clicked off and there was a loud humming sound, then a mechanical click as the gates started to open, the lock springing.

Frost started back toward the Mercedes, climbing inside, feeling slightly light-headed from the exertion, from just having stood. He started the Mercedes, cutting the wheel sharp left to get between the gates, glancing behind him in the rearview as he started up the graveled drive, seeing the gates closing shut after him. On the seat beside him under a raincoat he'd taken off Mahmed's hall tree was one of the Uzis, and all the loaded magazines he'd been able to steal from the bodies of the dead men. He hoped Mahmed had been right, that Reginald Field could be trusted.

Frost parked the Mercedes in front of the house. It was white, against the heat of the desert, and low, with a slightly peaked roof at the front, more the construction of a western ranch house than something he would have expected in North Africa. He could see the white car in the garage more clearly now. It was one of the old body design Rolls Royces, the kind with the design that had a 1930s flavor to it. He instantly liked it.

Frost started out of the Mercedes, seeing the front door of the house opening, a woman starting through. She had dark hair, auburn colored, was on the tall side, and slender appearing despite the billowing ankle length Arab style robe she wore. He could see her feet as she caught up the folds of the robe and started down the steps—she wore sandals.

"I told you I needed a man—Mahmed's heavy," Frost snapped, sounding angry to himself.

"I had to come instead."

"What about Reginald Field?"

"What about Reginald Field?"

"The mystery writer, the doctor—Mahmed's friend. Where is he?"

"You're looking at him," she smiled, then started toward the car. For the first time he noticed the small black medical bag in her left hand.

He called after her as she walked past him. "Reginald Field?"

"Yes," she sang back, not turning around, but starting to look into the back seat.

Frost leaned heavily against the right front fender of the Mercedes, mumbling half to himself, half aloud, "Wow—what they can do with sexual reassignment surgery these days! Whew!"

114

Chapter Twenty-Four

Frost opened his eye, staring up at the ceiling, seeing another of the omnipresent fans. He could smell the night desert air as he tried to sit up. His head suddenly ached. He leaned back. He seemed to find himself in strange beds with his clothes off on an almost regular basis, he reflected. But this time it was a couch, not a bed. He looked down across his body. A light afghan covered him, his right shoulder was stiff as he tried to move it and he looked down at it—it was heavily bandaged, and professionally so. His left hand, the web between the thumb and first finger, was bandaged as well.

He tried to sit up again, then heard the voice behind him, "I'd take it easy—that morphine shot I had to give you doesn't mix too well with whiskey—your breath smelled as though you were a tester in a brewery."

"How'd you guess what I do for a living," he smiled, trying to turn around to see her.

He couldn't, but he could hear the soft footfalls as she walked across the room, the rustling of clothing. She wore a long robe almost identical to the first one, but off white rather than pale blue. She obviously noticed his watching her, he thought. She lifted the robe slightly with the tips of her fingers and smiled down at him. "Got bloodstains all over the other one."

"How's Mahmed?"

"I got the bullets out—he should have been in a hospital, not here. But I know his work, and if he wanted to come here, that meant he couldn't go to a hospital. So, I don't know. We're the same blood type—I gave him a transfusion. If an infection sets in, he could have some problems. I'll know more tomorrow. How are you feeling?"

"Terrible," Frost smiled.

"Figured you might," she laughed. "I've never seen a man with so many scars—in some cases you have scars on top of scars—sort of a checkered pattern."

"Thanks a lot," Frost murmured, feeling woozy.

"Knife scars, bullet wounds, there's a big incision scar over your abdomen—"

"Mexico a while back—somebody submachinegunned me."*

"And your legs," she went on. "It looks almost as thought somebody tried skinning you—"

"Somebody did—but that was a while back too," Frost nodded.**

"You lead a dangerous life—are you a gunrunner like Mahmed, or shouldn't I ask?"

"I'm not a gunrunner like Mahmed—he's just an old friend. Was helping me with some information I

*See, They Call Me The Mercenary #2, *Slaughter Run*.

**See, They Call Me The Mercenary #3, *Fourth Reich Death Squad*.

needed—we have a mutual enemy."

"It looks as though your mutual enemy can be quite effective. Do you always go so heavily armed?"

It took Frost a minute—he was slow now because of the morphine, he thought. "What do—you—"

"That Uzi submachinegun on the front seat of the Mercedes—it was dirty, used a lot. And that 9mm pistol you had in your belt—and that little knife. A Gerber, isn't it? You see, I keep up on weapons for my books."

"What the hell happened after we got Mahmed up the stairs?"

"You passed out," she smiled, sitting on the edge of the couch near him, arranging her robe, not looking at him as she spoke. "You fainted, I guess. Loss of blood, shock. I dragged Mahmed the rest of the way. You're right—he is heavy, then I got him into bed. I went back and patched you up on an interim basis and left you on the floor in the hallway, then started to work on Mahmed. I worked all day on both of you—I just got to sleep a few hours ago—"

"Sleep—" Frost glanced at his watch. A day had passed according to the date.

"You were exhausted—you're pushing yourself too hard."

"How do you know so much about—"

"Bullet wounds and knife scars? I interned at a hospital in New York City. I did a lot of emergency room work. It always amused me that a city with such ridiculously strict laws governing ownership of firearms always had so many gunshot cases. I don't think their laws did much good."

"You won't get an argument on that from anybody

with common sense," Frost smiled. "Why Reginald Field?"

"You mean you've decided I'm not a sex change?"

"I wouldn't mind investigating it further."

She laughed, a healthy, throaty laugh that Frost instantly liked. "Well, I'm not—I was born with the same parts I have now—they've just altered a bit with time."

"I'm glad."

"I'm really Regina Meadows. A field and a meadow are close enough, and Regina and Reginald aren't far apart either. I felt people would be more inclined to take blood and guts murder mysteries from a man rather than a woman. And it's worked out nicely. I can go anywhere I want and never worry about reporters, anybody. I'm Regina Meadows—Reginald Field just exists on the books' covers."

"So long as they spell the name right on the check?"

"Exactly—and they do quite well. Your name is Frost—what do you do?"

"Mercenary soldiering, executive protection—right now though, I'm into something personal."

"You look tired," she smiled. "If you can help me, I can get you into one of the spare bedrooms and you can rest more comfortably."

"All right."

"I'd mention feeding you, but you'd get nauseated from it. Wait until tomorrow at breakfast. Come on—I'll help you up."

Frost started to sit, feeling her hands under his left shoulder and on his back. As he stood, the afghan covering him fell away. Suddenly, with the woman beside him, the smile on her face, the softness of her hands, he felt something—

"Don't be angry with yourself," she smiled, looking up at him. "That happens to men a lot with nurses and female doctors—sometimes you just touch a man in the—"

"Thanks," Frost smiled.

"It's all right—come on."

Frost stood there a moment, looking at her. "You're making me feel like I'm fourteen years old," he smiled.

"All men are fourteen years old," she laughed, getting his left arm across her shoulders and starting to walk with him.

"Remind me to punch you out, lady," the one-eyed man rasped.

"I like you too," she murmured.

Chapter Twenty-Five

Regina Meadows was apparently well connected, Frost had decided. Somehow, she'd gotten his luggage out of his hotel, notified the Don's man Alfonso and all of it without causing the police to knock at the door. He had no idea what she had done or had someone else do with the Mercedes, but it was gone, bloodstained seats and all.

He sat on the veranda, overlooking the balcony railing into the garden beyond. In the several days he had been staying at her home—Meadowshire, she called it—he had only seen one servant, a gardener, the man coming for three hours every morning in a battered pickup truck, then promptly leaving.

Aside from a good mystery writer, she was also a good cook, Frost had decided. He guessed her age at early to middle thirties, but was too polite to ask. And he liked her.

Frost sipped at a glass of icewater, watching the sun starting to set, hearing the by now familiar footfalls of sandals on the flagstones behind him.

"I decided your health could best be served with a drink," she said, setting down a silver tray on the glass topped table. On the tray was an icebucket, covered, two glasses and a bottle of scotch. She sat down to his right, sweeping the robe around her as she did. This one was pale yellow.

"I heard your typewriter going this morning," Frost said.

"I don't have a title for it yet."

"What's it about?"

She was putting ice in the glasses with a pair of tongs, but stopped and looked across at him for a moment. She looked away and finished with the ice, trying to open the fresh scotch bottle. Frost took it from her, twisting the top. "Women never open liquor bottles right—always try to peel them open. You just twist."

"Are you an expert on liquor bottles?"

"Whiskey, vodka, rum—I'm an expert. Used to be more of an expert."

"Tell me about yourself—I'm fascinated. I never met a mercenary before."

"Tell me about your book first?"

"All right," she smiled, leaning back, sipping at a glass of scotch. "It takes place in Switzerland—have you ever been there?"

"Yes," Frost smiled, remembering. He'd been there with Bess.*

"And do you ski?"

"Yes," Frost nodded, sipping at his own drink. After days without it, the scotch burned in his stomach. He shifted in his seat, his right arm, still in a sling to avoid aggravating the wounded shoulder, stiff.

"Well—I was only outlining, not writing the book,

*See, They Call Me The Mercenary #1, *The Killer Genesis.*

so I haven't got all the details worked out. But it takes place in Switzerland, at a clinic there. A man, an espionage agent, awakens in the clinic, completely immobilized, realizing he is being tested in preparation for surgery. He cannot talk, cannot move, cannot communicate with the doctors and the medical staff. He only knows where he is, but not why. So he tries to remember what happened to him so he can try to determine why he is there, what the surgery is all about."

"What's it all about?"

She smiled, warmly, enigmatically. "If I told you that, you wouldn't have to buy the book, would you?"

"Does that mean you don't know the ending?"

She smiled again, sipping at her scotch. "You've hung around writers before."

Frost nodded, smiling, trying to look enigmatic. He somehow didn't think he did it as well as she did. "How's Mahmed?" Frost asked, abruptly changing the subject.

"He's better this evening. By tomorrow morning, if you can talk with him very quickly, you should be able to ask him about that Chapmann woman. It sounds important to you."

"It is important. Is he resting now?"

"Yes—he's a strong man, despite his weight problem. I think he'll recover completely. But he should have bad scars, one of them especially bad on his back. I had to dig in rather hurriedly for the bullets."

"How did you know you had them all?"

"A good friend of mine—let's just say he gave me access to an X-ray machine he's been experimenting with for use in one of my books. It's portable. He never bothered to get it back, moved onto a newer prototype. It served my needs, though. I still consider myself a doctor, despite the fact I'm a writer." She smiled again, sipping at her drink, then asking, "Does that strike you as strange?"

"I haven't got the stomach for medicine. The only times I've pulled bullets out of guys I've felt sick to my stomach afterwards. Three things I could never be — a doctor, a dentist or a body snatcher."

"Body snatcher?"

"A mortician — can you see being down in some basement whacking apart dead guys to make 'em look good? Yuck!"

"You can fight, kill, all that and the thought of embalming someone sickens you?" she asked.

"Yep," Frost nodded. "Fighting's a fact of life — but that other stuff, takes a kind of guts I don't have and wouldn't want."

"Is that a compliment?" she smiled.

"I guess so," Frost nodded. "How come you live here, in the desert more or less? Write books? What made a woman become a doctor to begin with?"

"I liked playing doctor when I was a kid," she laughed.

"Tell me another one."

"How about, my father was a doctor and I wanted to follow in his footsteps?"

"I'd believe it if it's true," Frost told her, putting down his drink and lighting a cigarette.

"It is true, then."

"What made you switch professions?"

"Play detective — you read my books. Let's see if you

can guess," she smiled again, the enigmatic quality replaced by something almost little girlish.

Frost bent forward, his shoulder aching as he did, stubbing out his cigarette. "All right—I'll play. You wanted to be a writer, but felt you had to become a doctor to please your father—sounds like a soap opera."

"Not far wrong though. Then my father died and I realized that what I was doing wasn't what I wanted to do. I had a patient who was a New York publisher—I held my scalpel to his throat and made him read my first book and he bought it."

"I don't believe the part about the scalpel," Frost laughed.

"No—actually, I just asked him, and he read it, offered me a small advance and a healthy royalty. I didn't tell him I would have done it for free. He had kidney stones if I remember correctly."

"How are his kidney stones," Frost smiled.

"Better, last time we talked. He still pumps me for medical advice when we talk on the phone."

"You're an interesting woman," Frost told her.

"You're an interesting man," she answered, looking at him, her eyes—green—fixed on him.

"I'd like to go to bed with you—am I too direct?"

"Why do you think I brought out the scotch?" she smiled.

"I was hoping," the one-eyed man smiled.

"I hope you don't just like the missionary position," she smiled, sipping her drink. "I don't think your shoulder would take it."

"That's okay—there'll be a doctor near, right?"

"Yes," she said, her voice husky, good sounding.

Chapter Twenty-Six

"You were right about the shoulder," Frost told her, rolling over beside her.

"Let me," she whispered to him. "Relax—doctor's orders."

Frost felt her hands on his shoulder, rubbing the stiffness away. "Hell of a way to make love—right shoulder so bad I can't get on top, my left hand bandaged—I'm a wreck."

"No, you're not," she said, kissing his right ear. "See—your ear is fine, isn't it? There's a scar there—I can feel it."

"Guy tried biting it off once in a fight."

"What did you do?"

"Jabbed my knife into his crotch. He stopped trying to bite it off then."

"Violence—that's your life isn't it?"

"I guess—because it has to be. Doesn't mean I like it."

"If I tried biting off your ear would you, ahh—"

"I'd stab you with somethin' else," Frost smiled, hearing her laugh as he said it, feeling her teeth gnawing at his ear. "I mean it," he told her.

"I dare you," she whispered, then continued biting.

"You've got me at a disadvantage—"

"Wait a minute," she whispered, then rolled over on top of him.

"It defies gravity that way—it's unnatural," he said, faking seriousness.

"In my research for my novels, I always heard it was more difficult to shoot up at an angle than to shoot down."

"Depends on the situation," Frost laughed.

"Then you don't think it will affect your accuracy?" she whispered.

"Let's find out—okay?"

She just nodded, leaning her head against his chest. He felt her hands rubbing at him. "What are you doing?" he murmured.

"I'm just checking to see how easy it would be to give you a vasectomy—if I can feel for the—"

"Hey," and Frost started to move under her, then felt himself coming erect.

"Does that bother you?" she laughed. "I wouldn't do that unless you—"

"I don't," Frost told her, feeling her abdomen close against him as he came into her.

"Your voice wouldn't change or anything, and your beard would still grow—"

"I knew a guy who—ooh," and Frost hugged her closer to him. "Had it done—they use needles."

"Well—you're a grown up man—"

"I don't like needles," Frost confided, feeling her movement over him, around him.

"All right—I won't talk about it anymore."

"Good—besides, I've never been married."

"Legally, you mean," she whispered. He could feel

her body doing something, his own body doing it too.

"You always talk about operations when you—"

"No—just wanted to see what reaction you'd have," she whispered. "I was just test—"

"Shut up," and Frost drew her closer to him, pulling her face down to his with his right hand, for the first time tasting her mouth. It was warm, moist, and he liked it—very much.

He felt Regina Meadows shuddering against him after a moment, and he liked that too.

Chapter Twenty-Seven

Frost turned the water in the shower straight cold—
which wasn't terribly cold—and stood under it for a
moment, thinking about the woman, Regina Meadows,
about the meeting he would have in a few moments
with Mahmed, about the fact that he would soon leave.
He liked Regina Meadows, and oddly he thought she
genuinely liked him. It would be hard to leave.

He'd breakfasted with Regina before showering
earlier that morning, the two of them talking about
everything except the previous night for the longest
time, then finally, as she'd been getting up to get
more coffee, she'd blurted out, "Damnit—I love you,"
then walked off.

Frost thought about that a lot, what she had said,
how she had said it. He shut off the water, started out
of the shower and remembered he'd forgotten to dry
himself. He did that, studying his face in the mirror as
he combed his hair. He dressed in a pair of light
colored poplin slacks and a white shirt and a pair of
the Italian shoes.

Frost started out of his room, the bandage on his
right shoulder replaced with a smaller bandage, as
was the bandage on his hand. Silently, after breakfast,

Regina had replaced them, telling him finally that both wounds were healing and with a little exercise, the stiffness in his right shoulder would go away. She had left again, abruptly. He started down the narrow hall into the living room. Regina was sitting there, on the couch, her back to him.

He walked around the couch, seeing her turn to look at him, then look away. She wore one of her flowing robes again, this one light grey with a dark maroon pin striping.

He stood there a long moment, then finally asked her, "What's the matter?"

"Do you remember what I said at breakfast this morning?" She still didn't look at him.

'"Yes—I remember. I've been thinking about it a lot."

"Is that all you've been doing?" She turned her head fully away from him now.

Frost walked the few feet that separated them, put his hands on her shoulders and turned her around, drawing her up to him. She stood in front of him, the nipples of her breasts pressing against him through the fabric of the robe. He cocked her head up to him, so he could see her eyes. They were moist at the edges.

"It's not all I've been doing," he whispered, pulling her against him, his right arm, aching at the shoulder as he wrapped it around her, touching his mouth to hers. She pressed against him, away from him. He held her more closely until she sank against him, kissing him, crying openly now. Not knowing that it would be at all, he whispered it anyway, "It'll be all right . . ."

Mahmed looked somehow thinner than when Frost

129

had last seen him — a week, he thought? — earlier.

"My friend," the man murmured, looking odd without his red fez. But Frost thought he would have looked odder with it, in his sick bed. "You saved my life — I am forever indebted to you."

"Gimme twenty-nine ninety-five plus tax and we'll call it even," Frost quipped.

"Would that such a debt could be repaid so cheaply. I wished to tell you of the plans, the plans the Deathwitch has."

"Deathwitch?" Regina Meadows repeated.

"It's a kind of pet name for Eva Chapmann — if you knew her, you'd understand it."

"Hank — I don't like this," Regina whispered hoarsely.

Frost said nothing, but thought that neither did he.

Mahmed coughed once, and as Regina started to bend toward him, he waved her back. "And to you, Regina — I also owe my life. My two dearest friends now — and always," Mahmed whispered. "But the Deathwitch. She must be destroyed before she destroys us all. She wanted arms for Estaban Garcia-Ruiz. A fascist, a Nazi maybe — he — " Mahmed began to cough and Regina bent over him, Frost watching her slender silhouette against the bulk of the Arab.

After a moment, she turned to face Frost. "He can't exert himself anymore — I'm giving him a shot, to make him rest."

"All right," Frost told her, then walked out of the door into the hallway.

They sat on the veranda, sipping tea that tasted to Frost vaguely medicinal. "It's almond flavored — do you like it?" the woman asked.

130

"No—but I'm not much for exotic tastes."

"I see," she smiled. "You'd leave if you knew how to find Estaban Garcia-Ruiz, wouldn't you?"

"Yes," Frost told her. "I'd have to—no choice. Every day Eva Chapmann lives brings her closer to whatever it is she has planned. And eventually, if I don't get her, she'll find this house, kill us all—you too."

"Is she that evil?"

"More than I could ever describe. Just like her father."

"What happened to him?"

"I shot him to death," Frost told her matter-of-factly, lighting a cigarette to get rid of the taste of the tea.

"What are you going to do to her?"

"Shoot her, stab her, behead her—whatever I get the chance to do. I just want her dead. Period."

"Then what?"

"Gotta try and sort out my life," Frost told her.

"Can I be part of it or not?"

"I don't know—I don't know anything really. Except I've gotta do this."

"Will you come back—maybe?"

"This is very hard on you, isn't it?" Frost sighed heavily. "I'm sorry—I don't want it to be."

"There's a woman, isn't there?"

"Yes—her name is Bess."

"Is she waiting for you?"

"Yes—she always waits for me."

"She wants to marry you?"

"Yes."

"Do you want to marry her?"

Frost lit another cigarette with the butt of the last one, nodding, "Yes—but I don't know. I can't see myself married. I've really tried to see it that way. I don't know. But I love her."

"Do you love me?"

Frost looked at her, then nodded. "I think so—if I knew what I were doing, I guess we wouldn't have this problem, one way or another."

"Then come back to me if you solve it, Hank—I know how you can reach Mahmed's employer, Nikos Kalantos. Mahmed won't be strong enough to talk for some time yet, to really tell you what you need to know. I could keep you here that way, but I don't want to keep you here—that way, anyway. It's one of the little Greek-held islands—Chios. I have a friend who can get you there. He should be able to tell you about Garcia-Ruiz—Kalantos should."

"Why are you doing this?" Frost asked her, stubbing out his cigarette.

"Reasons of my own.'

"Bullshit—why?"

"I never told a man I loved him before. In my books, I make people do dumb things sometimes, because they love one another. Well, I guess I was reading people right all these years, or writing them right anyway. I'm doing something dumb. That's it."

"Thank you," Frost told her sincerely.

"Just do me a favor and we'll be square," she asked.

"What's the favor?"

"If you can come back and we can, ahh—"

'Otherwise don't come back?' Frost asked, looking at her.

"I'm glad you said it—I couldn't," she said and looked away over the veranda railing. Frost looked off toward the desert with her.

Chapter Twenty-Eight

Frost stepped down from the open fuselage door of the float plane, balancing himself on the starboard float with one foot, staring across the water.

"I got a rubber boat you can use, Yank," the British pilot shouted.

"Wonderful," Frost murmured. He could see a sentry, already studying him from the rocky cliff overlooking the white sandy beach less than five hunderd yards from the plane.

"Don't look friendly to me, they don't."

Frost glanced back to the Englishman. "Probably very friendly—just shy, that's all. You know how crippling shyness can be."

"You're right, I guess," the Englishman grinned, looking through the open fuselage door. "I betchya those blighters are even more shy."

Frost looked back toward the beach. Three Avon inflatables were coming out toward the aircraft, and in them men bristling with submachineguns. Frost heard a roar and looked up. Just coming over the false horizon created by the cliff was a sparkling new Sikorski gunship.

"Shy," Frost nodded. "Definitely shy—let's not frighten them," and slowly, Frost took his battered FN

High Power from his trouser belt, holding it up in the air with the tips of his fingers, raising his left hand skyward as well. "Shy," he sighed hard . . .

Frost walked up out of the surf, his expensive Italian shoes getting coated with sand and flooded with water. He could hear a radio crackling from one of the boats, but the helicopter had long since disappeared. Only two of the boats had come back toward the island, the third, with three submachinegun armed men, beside the plane, keeping Harry the pilot covered.

Frost stopped walking and turned around to the man nearest him, like the others armed with an Uzi. "You know," Frost smiled. "I'm beginning to think those things multiply like rabbits," and he gestured toward the subgun.

"It is a fine weapon."

"I know that," Frost smiled, slowly starting to lower his hands from behind his head.

"The hands—keep them—"

"Then go shoot me," Frost told the man. "And you'd better do it quick before I get out a cigarette and smoke all you guys. Smoke—get it?"

The Greek didn't laugh. Frost lowered his hands anyway, rubbing his still tender right shoulder. Slowly—he was more worried than he tried to appear—he reached into his pockets for his cigarettes and his lighter.

He flicked open the cowling of the Zippo, thumbed the striking wheel and lit the smoke. He could hear the helicopter again, but couldn't see it as he looked up. He could hear the radio crackling, a voice coming over it, but he couldn't tell the words over the noise of the unseen helicopter.

A man from the center of the four armed men beside the farthest rubber boat started walking toward Frost, Frost's FN High Power in his right fist.

"Your identity has been verified, sir."

Frost didn't know whether that was good or bad from the look in the man's black eyes. The man thrust the pistol forward, Frost almost swallowing the smoke from his cigarette. But then the man twisted the gunbutt around in his hand, extending the pistol further, toward Frost. Frost took it, slowly, the cigarette hanging in the left side of his mouth. He thumbed out the magazine, then jacked back the slide, catching the chambered round in the palm of his right hand. "You know," he began, reloading the pistol, "I have a terrific High Power—back stateside. Metalified, the action smoothed, the magazine safety deactivated. You'd love it." The man's eyes were still humorless. Frost took back his knife and the spare magazines for the pistol, pocketing them all. "You really would."

Frost mentally shrugged, mumbling as he started along the beach after the men that the dark eyed leader's lack of reaction was, ". . . Greek to me."

Chapter Twenty-Nine

Frost knew the smell now, having faintly detected it even from the plane when it had landed along the beach — a citrus smell from the orchards beneath him on the green plain of the island. He stood now, overlooking them as he waited for Nikos Kalantos to come.

Chios, Frost remembered, somewhere, vaguely, from something, held as its greatest claim to fame the production of mastik gum for the harems of the middle east. Aside from taste and breath freshening qualities, it also served as a mild tranquilizer. His one experience with what went on in a harem convinced him that tranquilizers could be of inestimable value to the master of a seraglio.*

"There is much to support the theory that Homer was born here."

Frost turned, looked behind him and saw the man who most certainly had to be Nikos Kalantos. "Homer? Homer who?"

"You jest, of course," the man said.

"Yes — I jest," Frost smiled. "And Delacroix — he made a painting having to do with some sort of fight here, didn't he?"

*See, They Call Me The Mercenary #7, *Slave of The Warmonger.*

136

"The massacre of 1822—it is an unpleasant subject. I thank you for saving the life of my valued friend Mahmed Aja."

"I value him as a friend as well," Frost answered.

"Ouzo—would you like that?"

"Not to be rude, but I'd prefer scotch or blended whiskey—anything like that."

The Greek gunrunner nodded soberly, clapped his hands and a woman, a black shawl covering her head, appeared. He said something to her and she left. "Do you speak our language?"

Frost had waited all his life for the line. "No—it's Greek to me—ha!"

Kalantos didn't laugh. "That is a very old joke, my mercenary friend."

"Sometimes I feel like a very old mercenary. An old joke is only fitting, I suppose."

"Mahmed has told me of you—you were a friend of the woman detective."

"Who saved your child—Julie—"

"Yes, Julie Pulman. But all my children are away from the island now, they have been since this thing with the Deathwitch first came about. Immediately I heard of the attack on Mahmed, all that I hold dear was taken to refuge. Please," the Greek smiled, gesturing toward a stone table at the center of the veranda, "come and sit—we will talk."

Frost lit a Camel, staring across the veranda, trying to decipher the man who was a modern legend in the gun smuggling business. He was short, wiry, dark of hair and eye, but obviously well past fifty. Not so much his appearance, but an air about him—it signalled age and some wealth of experience Frost had only heard rumored.

"I understand you are a true fighter—a lion, a killer when needed."

"I've been around," Frost nodded.

"I was like you when I was younger—ahh, here," and he stopped talking as the woman with the black shawl brought a tray with three bottles and two glasses. "You are American—do you require ice?"

"Water'll do," Frost nodded, seeing the pitcher on the tray, a towel draped over it.

"Very good—your pleasure?"

Frost eyed the three bottles—Smirnoff 100 Vodka, Canadian Club and Chivas Regal Scotch. Frost said, "The Canadian Club, please."

The woman seemed to understand the words and poured a glass half full with the whiskey, then added water to the top. Frost nodded and as she started to pour for Kalantos—the scotch—Kalantos said something Frost again could not understand and she left.

As Kalantos poured his own scotch, he remarked, "I fought with the British—I worked with them throughout the War—the real war, the one against Hitler. The bastard."

"I'll drink to that," Frost smiled.

They toasted glasses as Kalantos downed half his scotch. "Ahh—I confess I prefer whiskey to Ouzo, but it's expected of me to offer it. It's the Greek national beverage."

"Why here? I have to know," Frost asked, gesturing beyond the veranda, toward the island.

"You mean, why not Paris, or Monte Carlo? Very simple. My father died here. It was once fashionable for young men who were outlaws to become monks—a

138

way of dying with dignity. My father did this. I learned of him being my father only sometime after he had died. His body is interred in one of the monasteries on the far side of the island. Perhaps a very personal reason, but to me one that is sufficient. It is a lovely climate at any event. We are getting tourists. I may someday leave because of that."

"I came to learn what you know of Eva Chapmann's plans—so I can find her."

"And liquidate her? One man? In my prime, under optimum circumstances, I doubt I could have penetrated her defenses to kill her without aid. I doubt you to be capable of this either. But her plans, I can certainly inform you of those. They have to do with the old Spanish Fascist, Estaban Garcia-Ruiz. He is perhaps the most nationalist of the nationalists. I had no fondness for the Communists, but little fondness for the use of Hitler's Condor Legion, either. My older brother was a Communist—a fool, but a well intentioned one. He died in one of the Condor Legion bombings. But this Estaban Garcia-Ruiz—he hated everyone. He is very rich, and he is very ill. His last wish, apparently, is to push the British out of Gibraltar. The Spanish Government is more or less for this and has been for years. But not through violent means. Garcia-Ruiz, on the other hand, has always seen violent means as the only means. Therefore, he has hired Eva Chapmann and for some reason I cannot fathom, she wants British rifles and handguns, British equipment and British uniforms. And I understand she had been getting them."

"She has," Frost nodded soberly, sipping at his drink.

"Will you stay the night, and for dinner of course? I have an excellent cook and would relish the opportunity for her to prepare American food."

"Hot dogs?"

"I was thinking more of steaks—I'm afraid the island provisioners are very remiss at stocking hot dogs, potato chips, peanut butter—all sorts of American delicacies."

Both men started to laugh. "No taste at all," Frost remarked. "And no class either, those shopkeepers."

"I know—I frequently tell them that, so, what I need I smuggle in myself."

Frost laughed aloud, Kalantos asking, "What is so funny about a smuggler smuggling?"

"I was just thinking—take a crate and mark it 'submachineguns' and inside in a false bottom packed in dry ice you have chocolate milkshakes and tutti fruity ice cream."

Kalantos smiled—then laughed. "An interesting idea—I shall try it sometime to see if customs officials share your sense of humor."

Frost didn't think that they would.

Chapter Thirty

Frost pushed away from the table, full, the steak slightly well done for his taste, but satisfying nonetheless. He picked up his glass of Canadian Club, sipping at it as Kalantos finished the last of his own steak.

"Your cook is very good," Frost commented.

Kalantos, chewing as he talked — a habit he had demonstrated throughout the meal — nodded, saying, "Yes — but my wife is better. But because of this Eva Chapmann affair, my wife of course cannot be here."

"Have you tightened your security?"

"Startron scopes on all the approaches. I've mounted machineguns in the Sikorski you saw earlier. Each guard station has two men now rather than one, and I've laid up a supply of Laws rockets. Whether or not such precautions would do any good, I cannot say. Miss Chapmann seems to be a very determined woman. And it seems she not only wishes you dead, but wishes harm to my organization as well. With you here, I should say the likelihood of an attack, either tonight or tomorrow morning at the latest, is quite real."

"I agree," Frost nodded, then looking at the empty plates on the table, he asked, "Was this the hearty meal?"

"For the condemned men — possibly. Only time will

141

tell that. But one thing is certain. If we survive her attack, we must do something to foil her plans in Gibraltar. It would not be for the English as it was in the Falklands. Spain is a major military power in the Mediterranean, and were a war between England and Spain to be precipitated, the straits of Gibraltar bound up, I should think it could well precipitate a World War."

"Nuclear—"

Kalantos cut him off. "The closing of the straits of Gibraltar would certainly warrant it, I think. Both American and Soviet vessels would be cut off in the Mediterranean. It is not hard to imagine the unthinkable, is it?"

"No—I suppose it isn't," Frost admitted, lighting a cigarette.

"Tell me about this Sicilian Mafia leader of your acquaintance."

"You have a good intelligence network," Frost smiled. "There's not much to tell. Don Adolpho seems to be a decent man, despite his profession. His organization wants Eva Chapmann now for what happened to one of his men, a 'soldier' named Demetrius. He lost both his legs as the result of an ambush to get me. If what you're implying is what I think you're implying, I could possibly see an alliance. Possibly."

"You must think the way I do. If we warn Spain that something is afoot in Gibraltar, then Spain will begin a military buildup, which could bring about the war neither of us wants. If we warn England, the same result. If we warn U.S. interests, they may either bungle it or they will warn England and Spain, again bringing about the military buildup. If, instead,

Gibraltar awakens one morning to find a dead invasion army on its beaches, the invasion army clearly a band of rogue mercenaries under the leadership of a madwoman, well then that is a different matter."

"Do you have any idea what she might be planning—specifically?" Frost asked, lighting another cigarette.

"No—if there were Spanish uniforms and weapons involved, I might. The Spanish invade Gibraltar with a force of commandoes, etc. But with British weapons and uniforms, I can hardly—"

Frost sat bolt upright in his chair, the look on his face apparently what stopped Kalantos in mid-sentence, he thought. "I'm sorry—I just think I've put it together. And it's insane."

"What is it?" Kalantos asked, leaning forward, across the table.

"A replay of what her father did to my outfit back in Latin America, before I killed him—a massacre."*

"A massacre?"

"What if British commandoes crossed the border from Gibraltar into Spain, were apparently surprised and killed a bunch of women and children, civilians in general? Then what if the Spanish Army were tipped to what was going on and a vastly superior force encountered these British commandoes fresh from the massacre?"

"It would be an incident where neither side would believe the other—an immediate war footing."

"England would deny that the commandoes were British, and Spain would deny that its army had killed all the commandoes. But the press would pick it up,

*See, They Call Me The Mercenary #1, *The Killer Genesis*.

run with it and all of a sudden—"

"Too far to stop," Kalantos intoned.

"Too far to stop," Frost repeated. "She's got a bunch of guys she's going to dress up like British commandoes, send them across the border into Spain, have them commit some atrocity, then as they're withdrawing, the rest of her people will massacre the fake commandoes. A lot of carnage, no witnesses and then war between England and Spain over Gibraltar, the war Estaban Garcia-Ruiz wants to see happen."

"It is like something out of a nightmare."

"No," Frost said sombrely. "No—it's a typical Chapmann plan. She's just like her father. Every inch his daughter. The body count doesn't matter. Civilian atrocities don't matter. Nothing matters."

"Men like you and I—you sell death, I sell the tools with which to achieve it, yet like good merchants everywhere, we choose our clientele and reserve the right to withhold our services."

"Not Eva Chapmann," Frost said slowly. "Not Eva Chapmann." The one-eyed man downed the rest of his drink, almost sorry he realized what she planned. It was making him feel a little sick.

"You look pale, my friend. Your wound? It troubles you?"

Absently, Frost rubbed his right shoulder. "No—it doesn't trouble me—not my wound." He lit a cigarette, only after he'd lit it, realizing the previous cigarette was still burning in the ashtray. He stubbed it out. "It's a different wound entirely."

Chapter Thirty-One

Frost had showered, not knowing when his next chance might be, then laid out clothes and weapons beside his bed, ready. He had tried getting his mind clear enough to sleep by reading another book by "Reginald Field" — but the female character only reminded him of Regina Meadows. He'd put the book down.

Sleep had come, but during the night several times he had awakened, remembering how it had been when his own outfit had been slaughtered under Eva Chapmann's father's orders. He remembered it all and it made him sweat to think of it.

He awakened again, the black luminous face of his Rolex reading nearly five-thirty — too early, but he got up and showered once more, realizing sleep was impossible.

After a long time under the cold water, he got out, toweled himself dry and marched barefoot across the room to the edge of the bed. He sat down to pull on his socks — Eva Chapmann would come today, he realized. Perhaps not Eva herself, because she would be busy planning her attack on Gibraltar, perhaps ready to carry it off, perhaps not yet. But her men would come, to kill him and to kill Kalantos.

Frost stood up and pulled on his underpants, then a pair of Levis, and a pair of deck shoes. He found a shirt and pulled it on.

He checked his weapons. There was the FN High Power he had gotten from the Don, loaded, a half dozen spare magazines for it loaded as well. There was his Gerber knife, the MkI boot knife. From Kalantos, he had borrowed an Uzi, in case the attack should come in the middle of the night as a surprise. For the Uzi, there were six spare magazines as well, these in a musette bag made of canvas.

He stuffed the High Power into his trouser band, all but decided to leave the Uzi in his room as he went into the main portion of the house to seek out breakfast.

It was a quarter past six as he glanced at his watch. The explosion didn't rock the building, shatter the glass, or do anything dramatic in his immediate vicinity.

But he heard it, and he knew what it was. He had the musette bag slung diagonally, cross body to his left side, the Uzi in his right hand, his left hand on the knob of his bedroom door as he heard the running in the hallway. He opened the door, seeing Kalantos at the far end of the hallway, running toward him. Kalantos' hair was wild from sleep, his dark complexion darker with a heavy growth of beard, a pair of rumpled khaki bush shorts all that he wore except for deck shoes, like Frost himself wore.

"The attack—she has come. They are raiding the village."

Frost almost said, "Good." But he started running back after Kalantos instead . . .

The streets of the village were visible as Frost, Kalantos and two dozen of Kalantos' men started down the steep grassy incline; and in the village streets, Frost could see fatigue clad men with submachineguns and assault rifles, running, torches in their hands, some of the houses in the village already ablaze.

"This is only to draw us away from the main house," Frost shouted, breathless with the running.

"I know that," Kalantos shouted back, jumping over a hummock of ground. There was a citrus orchard separating Kalantos' estate from the village and Frost, Kalantos and the others started into it, running between the orange trees, the wrinkled fruit that had hit the ground and fallen from the trees smelling strong and fetid, mingling with the burning smell coming from the village. The smoke was thickening as they crossed the orchard, and beyond the smoke, Frost could see movement.

"Get down!" the one-eyed man shouted. "Hit the dirt!" Frost dove behind the meager shelter of one of the skinny trees, firing his Uzi at a fatigue clad figure running from the smoke. The figure toppled back into the smoke.

There was gunfire all around him now. Kalantos was shouting commands in Greek, a half-dozen of his men maneuvering at a right angle to Frost's far left, along the boundary of the citrus grove, disappearing after a few seconds into the smoke.

There was heavy gunfire from beyond the smoke, screaming. Then Kalantos shouted something in Greek, but oddly, Frost felt, he somehow understood it, thinking that perhaps every fighting man anywhere understood it regardless of the words in which the command was spoken. "Follow me!"

Frost was up, running, a half-dozen of Kalantos' men

with him, penetrating the smoke barrier at the far end of the citrus grove. He half stumbled, catching himself. It was a body, fatigue clad, sprawled along the ground, the throat ripped out with a knife or machete.

He eyed the dead man once, then pushed himself up and kept running. Kalantos' men played for keeps, he decided.

Out of the smoke, he could see the village clearly again, fighting in the streets, farmers and shopkeepers, men and some women, defending their homes with clubs and sticks and butcher knives, Eva Chapmann's mercenaries stalled near the center of the village.

And between the village boundary and the edge of the citrus grove where Frost stopped, he could see perhaps two dozen more of Eva Chapmann's mercenaries, withdrawing toward the village, firing as they ran.

Frost caught Kalantos' face and both men looked at one another. "I need one of them alive — we've got to."

"But only one," Kalantos rasped.

"They'll be attacking your house."

"There will be time to get them there."

Frost nodded, pointing to six of Kalantos' men to follow him. "Take this man, Ari — he speaks some English," Kalantos shouted. Frost started to run then, toward the center of the village and the main street which ran toward it, the man Ari — broad shouldered, and almost oddly for a Greek badling baldy — running beside him.

"Tell 'em to stop that man — the one with the torch," Frost shouted, spraying his Uzi toward one of the Chapmann mercenaries.

Frost heard something that sounded like "Piyasteh ton," and he looked at Ari, but only shrugged, deciding it was the right thing whatever it meant. The man with the torch went down in a fusillade of subgun fire from Frost's men.

Frost started to run again, perhaps as many as a dozen — he wasn't able to count them accurately — of Eva Chapmann's men diving over a small embankment a hundred yards ahead of them, opening fire.

"Get the men down," Frost shouted to Ari, hitting the dirt as the ground around them chewed up under submachinegun fire. Frost was firing his Uzi toward the position, the men around him doing the same. "Pinned down," Frost shouted to the big, balding Greek."

"Not down," Ari nodded reassuringly — "Keeta!"

"Key-top?"

"Keeta — look, look!"

Frost followed the upward extended left hand, not hearing over the noise of the gunfire, but coming over the false horizon of the walls surrounding part of Kalantos' house he could see the Sikorski.

Frost could feel his cheeks seaming, his mouth upturning with a smile. "Translate for me, Ari," Frost said to the big Greek. "Tell the guys, let's murder those suckers!"

Frost started to his feet, a fresh stick in the Uzi, hosing it toward the enemy position. Frost heard something, a man shouting behind him. He couldn't understand the words — something like "Prosohee!"

Frost kept running, hearing the strange word again, then Ari's voice, loud, clear, and shouting, "Look out, captain!"

Frost wheeled to his right, two of the Chapmann

149

mercenaries coming out of a patch of scrub brush, submachineguns in hand. Frost rolled right, already firing. But the first man was already going down as Frost sprayed the second man in a long, ragged burst, Frost rolling across the ground.

Frost pushed himself to his feet, swapping sticks in the Uzi and starting to run again, toward the village street. There was submachinegun fire, assault rifle fire—the cracking sounds heavier, more ringing on the dank and smoke filled air.

A long archway started the street and Frost, Ari and four of the original six men Frost had taken with him, reached the archway. Beyond it ornate iron grillwork balconies, the undersides of the balconies as ornate as oriental rug patterns, the white walls etched in gold-colored mosaic patterns.

A dozen of the Chapmann mercenaries were fifty yards beyond the archway, firing toward Frost and his position. Frost edged along the archway wall, chips of stucco and masonry dust spraying at his face and hands as the subgun slugs impacted along the wall.

Frost pulled back, the ricochetting sounds of the submachinegun fire maddening. "Ari," the one-eyed man shouted.

"Neh"

"Yes—right?"

"Neh," the big, balding Greek nodded.

The one-eyed man smiled. "Get your guys to lay down the heaviest fire they can, and you and I run toward those balconies. You give me a leg up to the one nearest the archway and have your men keep up the covering fire as you join them. I'm going to use those balconies like a ladder, to make for the roof line.

With this," and Frost gestured with the Uzi, "and my pistol, I can make it hot enough down there for them to flush 'em out, into a killing ground for you and the others."

Ari nodded.

Frost nodded, changing sticks on the Uzi, then taking his empties and signalling with them to the other men—instantly each man was offering him a fresh magazine. Frost took three, giving him six thirty-two round magazines, just what he'd started with, plus one magazine already loaded into the weapon.

He looked at Ari, the big Greek extending his hand. Frost took it. "Let's go."

Ari grumbled a long string of what sounded to Frost like commands, the four remaining men splitting, two to each side of the archway. Ari was making some sort of series of hand signals now as Frost slung the Uzi diagonally across his back, muzzle down.

He tried judging the height of the nearest balcony. The one eight or so feet beyond it was lower, easier to reach, but farther out into the no man's land of gunfire. He couldn't risk it.

Ari was beside him now, edging as close as they dared toward the end of the tunnel-like archway. Frost pointed with his right hand, toward the near balcony, and Ari nodded. Then Frost raised his right foot, then cupped his hands together, pointing toward Ari. The big man nodded—almost grimly—once.

Ari shouted something in Greek, the four men, two on each side of the stuccoed archway, flat against the walls, the forward men kneeling, the rear men standing, their Uzis held in an assault position. There was another command and the four men started

151

firing, toward the Chapmann position beyond the open street and the balconies, behind an overturned crate and in the shelter of a low masonry wall more like a fence, surrounding overturne tables and a still burning Cinzano umbrella that had once shielded patrons from the sun.

There was another signal from Ari, and simultaneously, the big Greek tapped Frost on the left shoulder. The firing from the right side of the archway—nearest the balconies—stopped. Ari, Frost behind him, ran toward the nearest balcony.

The big Greek flexed his knees, feet wide apart, his hands supported in front of him like a stirrup, Frost three paces behind him. Frost jumped, his left foot catching up in the cupped hands of the Greek, his hands reaching upward as the Greek hurtled him toward the balcony.

Frost's right shoulder ached—if it had had a voice it would have screamed, he thought. But his fists were midway on the grillwork of the balcony railing, and the Greek was still elevating him. Frost reached his left hand—stronger now—up toward the top of the balcony railing, his left foot pulling up, the toe of his deck shoes scratching against the masonry base of the balcony beneath the railing.

He could hear the chattering of subgun fire beneath him, averting his right eye as a burst of automatic weapons fire hammered into the base of the balcony.

As Frost started up, over the railing, he glanced downward once, hearing a muted scream. Ari—his body was half sprawled against the house wall under the balcony, his left arm hanging limply at his side, but the Uzi spraying from his right hand.

Frost flipped the balcony railing, tucking down under a hail of gunfire, glancing back and downward again, seeing two of the gunrunner's men going for Ari. Frost flattened himself on the balcony floor, ramming the stubby muzzled Uzi ahead of him, between the ornamental curves of the iron grillwork, firing down on the Chapmann men. A three round burst—one of the men, fleeing the burning Cinzano umbrella as it collapsed downward on him, went down dead. Frost fired again, a long, hosing spray, catching one of the Chapmann men in the left leg and abdomen, a second man twisting, lurching forward, his subgun firing into the ground as his neck spurted blood.

Frost looked behind him again. Ari, feebly with his left hand, was signalling to Frost to go on. The one-eyed man shouted—in English—"Keep me covered," then edged back to the rear of the balcony nearest his covering fire.

He fired a burst with the Uzi, then let it swing onto his back as he reached upward for the lowest portion of the next balcony, starting already to prop his right foot on the top of the rail. He pushed himself up, gunfire hammering into the grillwork, the sound of the bullets pinging, metal against metal, almost deafening.

His right fist, then his left locked on the balcony railing above and he swung out, gunfire tearing into the stuccoed wall beside him. He hauled up his right foot, slipped and started to fall, catching himself on his hands, his feet swinging in mid-air. More gunfire, chunks of the stuccoed wall falling on him, the dust almost choking him as some of the masonry underneath powdered, showering his face. He squinted his good eye against it, getting his left foot up onto the balcony base, then pushing himself up, flipping the rail and hitting hard on the balcony floor.

Gunfire tore into the glass of the balcony doors behind him, shards of glass and strips of wood pummeling him, covering his back and his arms.

Frost edged forward on the balcony. There was air space of about four feet to the balcony over the adjoining structure, the balcony itself about four feet higher at the base. The gunfire came again, heavier this time.

Frost timed it, hearing the answering gunfire from his covering force, below and behind him. Frost fired a burst from his Uzi, emptying it into a running Chapmann mercenary starting to flip the low, fence-like wall of the outdoor cafe. The man caught it in mid-air, twisting violently, then falling flat, unmoving.

Frost rammed a fresh stick up his subgun, then started for the railing, getting his right foot on it, then his left, supporting himself against the wall.

More gunfire, more chunks of stucco and masonry disintegrating around him, more shattering of glass.

He stretched out his hands, shouting—mad, he wondered of himself?—"I can fly, you bastards!" He jumped, his hands reaching out for the balcony railing across the airspace, both fists wrapping around it.

He felt himself smiling, then felt nausea in the pit of his stomach. The balcony railing was pulling away from the masonry, starting to bend out toward him, his grip loosening as he started to plummet downward. Frost loosed the railing, feeling the wrought iron grillwork as it hammered against his shoulder and back, brushed against the side of his head. As his fingers curled over the masonry edge of the balcony base, he could feel blood trickling down the side of his head, near where his left eye had been. "Wonderful," the one-eyed man rasped, feeling his fingers slipping, the masonry surface near his fingers dissolving under the impact of subgun fire, the windows below him shattering as bullets pelted through them.

Frost clawed with his right hand, throwing his splayed fingers across the edge of the balcony, searching for a purchase, the friction of his arm against the masonry all that held him now. The one-eyed man looked below him — the drop was more than thirty feet.

His left hand was going numb and the fingers slipped. His hand scraped against the masonry, his right hand slipping now too. The front railing, facing the street, was his only chance. He let go with his left hand, reaching instead for the railing, his fist balling around it, the railing starting to sag under his weight. More bursts of subgun fire. But his right hand was on the railing now and he swung his body to the side, like a pendulum, his fists tightening on the grillwork as his left leg swung up. The masonry beside his left foot chewed and disintegrated under the impact of a burst of automatic weapons fire. His foot slipped. Frost swung his body again, his left foot getting a purchase once more. There was more gunfire, but ripping into the stucco wall instead, beneath and above him. Frost got his left leg all the way onto the ledge of masonry, then heaved himself up, toward the railing, half flipping, half falling over it. He stumbled to the balcony floor, another heavy burst of automatic weapons fire hammering a ragged line along the wall, the stucco powdering, spraying his face.

A massive plant in a hanging basket shattered above him, dirt and muddy water and plant material—dead leaves—falling across his back.

But Frost twisted his body around on the platform of masonry balcony, keeping flat. He was high enough now and he raised the muzzle of the Uzi. He could see at least a half-dozen of the Chapmann men on the street below him.

"Eat lead you bas—" Frost fired the Uzi, not trying for accuracy, but instead burning through the magazine, spraying the street below him, at the massive target area—the stuccoed walls, the fence-like low masonry wall where the cafe courtyard met the street, the tables and chairs, the glass front of the window behind the courtyard, the hanging plants, the balled and bagged cheeses, the rattan wrapped wine bottles—all of it shattering, splintering, exploding under the impact of the full metal case slugs as he fired the Uzi.

The Uzi's barrel smoked as he rammed a fresh stick in place and continued to fire. His left hand brushed against bare metal for a moment, the skin sticking to it, tearing as he moved his hand away, the burned area blistering as he re-grasped the weapon and continued firing.

Frost changed sticks again, catching sight of his own men—the big balding Greek was with them, his left arm limp at his side still—coming out of the protection of the archway, firing, their subguns in an assault position.

Frost changed sticks again. The bulk of the Chapmann mercenary force still in the village was making a last charge—eighteen men perhaps. Frost didn't have the time to count them exactly. Frost fired

156

out the magazine, then changed again, the action slowing with the built up powder residue, the smell of the oil in the moving parts burning with the heat of the sustained fire, acrid smelling as he kept firing in spite of it. Hot brass pelted his face and chest and hands, the brass burning his skin, some of the empty brass flying into his shirt.

Frost changed sticks again. Seven or eight men were still on their feet, firing.

Frost pumped the Uzi, shattering a wooden flower cart, killing two of the Chapmann men. He kept firing, a massive chunk of the masonry barrier surrounding the sidewalk cafe splitting away. One of the Chapmann men screamed, tumbling over it, his head split above the eyes by submachinegun fire or spraying debris.

Frost fired toward two running men, one of them going down, spinning, going flat on the bleached white street, his blood seeming to pour out in a tiny stream toward the gutter. The second man spun, firing, and Frost pumped the Uzi—it was empty. The wall behind his head was powdering as the one-eyed man grabbed at the High Power and dropped the thumb safety, pulling the trigger once, then once more, then once again. The subgunner suddenly stopped firing. There was no firing from the street below, but in the distance back near the house, Frost could hear gunfire and explosions.

The Chapmann man stood there in the street, the Uzi falling limply from his hands. He was perfectly erect. Frost stood up on the balcony, watching the Greek gun-runner's men standing stock still in the street below him as well.

The Chapmann man took a half step then, falling flat on his face. And the body never moved again.

Chapter Thirty-Two

Frost ran from the orange grove, Nikos Kalantos beside him, the big balding Greek—Ari—running slightly behind. Up at the top of the rise in ground hundreds of yards away yet, Frost could see running men, bursts of gunfire coming from the rocks and the walls of the house, the helicopter, its machineguns blazing, sweeping from side to side over the no man's land between the house walls and the attacker's lines.

The smoke in the orange grove had largely cleared, but there was smoke ahead of him now, billowing up from a portion of the house roof, far beyond the walls.

Frost stopped, glancing from right to left, counting the men remaining of Kalantos' force that had gone to the rescue of the burning village, the flames there behind them still leaping skyward. Eight men remained, not counting Frost himself, Kalantos and Ari.

"Eleven of us," Frost rasped to Kalantos.

"Down," the Greek gunrunner murmured, gesturing to his men and saying something Frost didn't understand. The Greek reached under his left shoulder, snatching a Heckler & Koch P-7 loose of the leather, then looked at Frost. "What is it you suggest, Captain Frost?"

"Get that helicopter to stop defending the wall and

strafe their position, pin 'em down while we advance. We close with 'em, kill 'em—but we still need one alive. An officer or a senior NCO."

"Agreed—a good plan for the spur of the moment." Then Kalantos turned to Ari, saying something Frost didn't understand. The big Greek produced a flare pistol—an H-K—from the musette bag hanging at his left side. Kalantos took it from him, broke it open like a shotgun, then took the flare Ari handed him. He loaded the pistol, murmuring, "I have planned for such a day as this—a red starburst flare indicates to the helicopter pilot to reposition himself. The selection of the next flare determines in what mode. A green starburst will send him to pin down any attackers."

"Plan ahead—I like that," Frost nodded.

"I thought that you would," Kalantos smiled, firing the first flare. Frost watched it sail into the sky, trails of smoke from the flare crisscrossing the smoky vapor trails in the air from the village fire and the fire at the house.

The helicopter abruptly began to break contact as the starburst—red—broke.

Already, Frost could hear the sound of the H-K flare pistol being broken open, reloaded and closed. "Guns, knives—whatever it takes," Frost murmured.

"Agreed," Kalantos rasped, "and now the green!" Frost heard the pop, the whoosh and saw the flare going airborne, saw it burst, the green starburst's ignition acting like a switch on the helicopter. The Sikorski started out over the wall, a hail of gunfire surrounding it as it swept low over the Chapmann attackers' position. Frost could see a LAWS rocket

159

being fired toward the Chapmann position, but from the wall.

"Let's go," Frost snapped, Kalantos nodding, shouting something in Greek and Frost, Kalantos and the nine other men suddenly on their feet, running.

Frost had two Uzis, the one he'd used on the balcony in the village left behind, traded for two more gently used models. As he stalked forward, he fired both, alternately, pinning down the Chapmann people as the helicopter strafed them from above.

There was stray small arms fire coming as they advanced, but Kalantos, Ari and the others were firing as well, the helicopter finishing its pass, spinning in mid-air and making another sweep. The distance to the enemy position was less than a hundred yards, and Frost broke from his jog trot into a dead run now, shouting something neither English nor Greek, but rather something from inside him, more like a primitive man's war cry.

Fifty yards and Frost's Uzis were empty. He dropped them to his sides and took his High Power pistol and a second High Power snatched from the dead body of one of the Chapmann mercenaries.

Twenty-five yards. Frost was shooting, first the gun in his right hand, then the one in his left, then the right.

The small arms fire from the Chapmann position was abating.

Ten yards, and Frost shouted again, but this time in English. "Kill 'em!"

They closed.

Frost fired both pistols point blank into the face and chest of a Chapmann man coming at him with an Uzi. Frost snatched up the Uzi, hosed it out toward a knot of six men, then threw the empty subgun at another man, starting to fire his pistols again.

Two men were rushing him, one with an assault rifle—Frost didn't catch the make—but at the muzzle was a long thin bayonet.

Frost fired out his pistols, slowing the man with the bayonet, killing the other. The man with the bayonet kept coming. Frost sidestepped, his little boot knife in his right fist, and as the man with the bayonet charged, passed him and missed, Frost was on him, hammering the knife into the man's back, bulldogging him to the ground.

Frost heard, felt—something. He rolled, his knife gone, his pistols gone. A man was lunging toward him, a machete in his right hand, swinging.

The one-eyed man reached into his shirt pocket, snatching the black felt tip pen—The Scribe—now his only weapon. He unscrewed the cap, the icepick-like triangular blade close against his wrist.

The man with the machete lunged, Frost sidestepped and shoved his right arm out to full length, like a fencer holding a rapier, the little hideout push dagger plunging lethally into the carotid artery on the right side of his opponent's neck.

Frost could hear one man screaming and he knew why—a captured Chapmann man and Ari or some of the others, perhaps Kalantos himself, would be carving on him, to make him reveal plans for the Deathwitch's assault on Gibraltar.

There was a long scream, hideous sounding and the one-eyed man started to walk away. For the scream had meant the man had talked and was now no longer breathing.

Chapter Thirty-Three

Hank Frost sat on the veranda of the Don's Sicilian home. There were more guards than he had remembered, but he supposed it was because of the Deathwitch. It was always possible she would be insane enough to attack the home of the principal Sicilian Mafia Don—something not even a fool would do, Frost knew. But with Eva Chapmann, anything was possible.

He heard footsteps behind him, and for a moment was back in the outskirts of Tangier with Regina Meadows on a similar veranda. He closed his eye, shook his head, then lit a cigarette, feeling a smile coming to his lips. . . .

He glanced behind him, standing then. Constanza, the Don himself and Nikos Kalantos. "Well?" Frost asked, seeing Constanza smiling at him.

"At the insistence of my headstrong niece, since I cannot accompany you in this mission, she will represent my organization. But if she dies, I will hold you both responsible," the Don concluded.

"What?" Frost asked.

"We are going to stop your Eva Chapmann," Constanza said brightly. "All of us. My uncle's men, Signore Kalantos' men, you and me—to stop her before she starts a war."

"You can't come," Frost snapped, seeing the wariness in Kalantos' eyes.

"I come or no army," she smiled back. "The Kalantos men—they are not enough, they have been badly cut by this last attack on Chios. You have no choice. My uncle—he will give you two hundred men, all armed and good fighters. Signore Kalantos says he has fifty men, and the heavy equipment. And you are an experienced soldier. We will triumph."

"Horse—" Frost cut himself off, not knowing how the old Don felt about profanity.

But the Don smiled. "She will observe only—and from a position of safety."

Frost looked at the girl, her dark eyes gleaming, her dark hair shining, the pale pink sundress she wore against her suntanned skin. He looked back at her eyes.

Something in her eyes said she planned more than observation from a safe distance, something more like actual fighting. He didn't need it, to have someone to look out for. But he needed the men the Don could provide. As Frost nodded, shaking the Don's hand, Frost mentally debated how angry the old gentleman would be if he decked the man's niece with a short right to her pretty jaw.

Chapter Thirty-Four

Kalantos' gunsmith had made Frost the gun he'd requested. A civilian CAR-15 barrel and collapsible stock with a M-16 receiver. Selective fire, it provided for the one-eyed man the best of both worlds. Atop the carrying handle, Frost had ordered mounted a standard Colt three power scope. He stood atop the deck of Kalantos' fifty-foot cutter, waiting for the final word now. The straps of two musette bags crossed his chest and back, in one spare magazines for the "CAR-16" as Frost called it, and in the other spare magazines for the Uzi slung across his back and the two FN High Power pistols on his belt.

A third bag — a gas mask bag sans gas mask — carried fragmentation grenades, this across his chest.

The moon above him was most of the time obscured by the patches of clouds which dominated the night sky, but when the moon was free of them, the surfaces of the water reflected its light, like tiny diamonds.

He smoked a cigarette, leaning against the rope rail in the bow pulpit of the ship, hearing footsteps behind him, turning.

It was Constanza.

"What is that big knife on your belt?"

"A Gerber Mk II — fighting knife. The best. Why?"

"I'll have to requisition one."

Frost eyed her up and down, smiling as he thought about it—eyeing was all he could ever do, since he had only one. She wore clothes much the same as his, but he realized they looked much better on her. Frost's face itched from the cammie makeup. But it looked almost appealing on her.

"I'll knock you down, knock you out—"

"Not up?"

"You've got a dirty mind."

"I'm still going—maybe the fighting will purge me."

"If I cold-co—scratch that," he smiled, almost embarrassed. "If I knock you out and leave you here, you won't have any choice. And I'll do it if I have to."

She smiled. "I studied karate."

"Good," Frost smiled back. "It'll keep you from hurting yourself when you fall."

"You wouldn't hit the niece of a Don—and besides, I can handle a submachinegun as well as any man."

"Good —you'll have to show me sometime."

"I'm going."

Frost shrugged, then flashed his right fist outward, catching her chin—as gently as he could—and then scooping her into his arms as she passed out.

Alfonso was coming along the companionway, rushing toward them. "Signore Frost!"

"She'll be fine," Frost assured him.

"But the niece of the Don, Signore!"

"It's okay—most women have a glass jaw anyway." Frost shouldered past Alfonso and started to take the unconscious girl inside. Her face, streaked with cammie makeup, caught the glow of the sheltered running light on the companionway steps, a yellow cast on her skin. But he thought she was beautiful.

Chapter Thirty-Five

"If we survive this, my friend, the old Don may kill you—I fought with him during the war for a very short time. He is a tough man, one of the toughest fighters I have known."

Frost smiled at Kalantos, seeing the Greek's face fleetingly in a shaft of moonlight as the cloud cover broke. "What do you mean—the old Don, mad at me?"

"She was unconscious and her wrist was handcuffed to the lavatory pipe in her cabin—he will be angry."

"Naw," and Frost shook his head. The Don's anger—at least for the moment—was his last concern. Frost listened instead to the waves lapping against the sides of the Avon inflatable boat.

The carefully agreed upon scenario they were relying on Eva Chapmann to follow was complex, but so far, it seemed to be paying off, Frost reflected. Like clockwork the freighter the Don's union personnel had located as Eva Chapmann's mobile base had pulled out of the docks, and while it was making the several hundred mile journey, Frost had worked with the Don's men, training experienced street fighters and gunmen to behave at least slightly like soldiers—the fundamentals of envelopments, small unit tactics for fire and maneuver elements, whatever he thought might be useful considering the terrain where the fighting would be.

Frost glanced at the luminous black face of his watch, rolling back the cuff on his sweater. Precisely an hour earlier, her ship had dropped anchor just outside the territorial waters of Gibraltar and motorized launches had been set out for the coast. One of the U.S. friendly mid-east nations to whom Kalantos supplied small arms and night vision equipment had agreed to an unofficial high altitude overflight of the coastal area and using night vision equipment Kalantos had supplied for free, snapped photos of the anchorage, then of the launching of the small boats. According to his best judgment, he would hit the beaches ten minutes ahead of her force.

Her force would be wearing British uniforms and ready to penetrate across the border between Spain and Gibraltar. The Don's intelligence had confirmed the location of the town to be hit by the men disguised as British commandoes. With luck, Frost thought, the men would never get there and no one in the sleepy Spanish town would even have a fitful sleep over it.

There would be twenty-five minutes before the second Chapmann landing party would come ashore, at least judging by the spacing of the launches from the freighter as confirmed by a third high altitude pass. These would be the men the first party assumed were here as back up in case of unexpected resistance, but who, in reality, were there to slaughter every man in the first party and make certain that no one in the surprised village was alive either. Frost was certain of her plan and had been since he'd realized it, but Kalantos had confirmed the last loose end for him.

Spanish marked 7.62mm CETME assault rifles had been stolen from an arsenal outside Madrid. These would be used by the second landing party, some of them left behind as "evidence" of the contact between Spanish and British troops. And the deaths of an entire Spanish village to the last man and an entire, although fake, company of British commandoes, to the last man, would be all Estaban Garcia-Ruiz needed to bring about his war between Spain and England over custody of Gibraltar.

The shore line, a gray blur there in the darkness where the land and water met, was less than two hundreds yards off and Frost checked his weapons one last time.

With the ninety-six men coming ashore in the first party, guns would only be a last resort, for the noise of gunfire would carry out to sea and warn away the second landing party. That could not happen.

Frost could hear the breakers now, loud as they crashed against the rocky beach. The noise would be to his ultimate advantage. . . .

It was going to be bloody business, the one-eyed man thought, crouching in the shadows, behind the rocks. His musette bags were gone, as was his assault rifle and the Uzi. He wore his pistols, but only perfunctorily. Unless an impossible situation arose and his only means of saving his life was a gun, he would not use one. He had both of his knives, the big one and the little one he always carried, and earlier, before the first landing party had come ashore, he had given each one a last touch of the sharpening steel.

"They are preparing to set out," Kalantos whispered in Frost's right ear.

The one-eyed man merely nodded, his smaller knife slipping back into its holster in the small of his back, the larger one in his right hand.

Frost tugged three times on the black silk cord behind him. The cord ran the length of the crescent shaped formation the mixed force of Sicilian Mafioso and Greek gunrunners waited in, each man with standing orders to keep one hand on the cord, the cord taut so that the slightest vibration would register along its length on both sides.

Then each man was to count to ten, while selecting his first target, then move out.

There was little danger that the nearly one hundred men on the beach would break out their weapons. Gunfire would alert British forces near the coast and would scare off the second landing party, whom the men of the first landing party would consider reinforcements.

Frost had soul searched, more than he had thought that he would. His aim was to kill every man on the beach, haul off the bodies and wait for the second landing party. He had considered the possibility that what he planned was perhaps on a level with what Eva Chapmann herself had planned as the fate of these men. The thought had disturbed him, but then he had reasoned through it. If the men lived they would slaughter the Spanish village of Campo de Morales. Three hundred people lived there.

And these men had been willing to do that.

Frost counted out to ten, his target already acquired.

He was up, moving as soundlessly as he could across the rocks and sand in his combat booted feet, the fingers of his right hand clenched on his knife through the fingerless cloth gloves he wore.

The target wore the uniform of a British captain. Frost was within ten yards of the man before the man wheeled, reaching for his gun.

Frost stopped, cold, touching the first finger of his left hand to his lips, saying, "Shh!"

The fake British commando reached instead for his Fairbairn-Sykes style knife, then edged forward, wicked-looking — Frost thought — a smile lighting his face. Frost stepped back as the "captain" shouted across the beach. "Can't be too many of them lads — cut 'em — no guns!"

Frost hefted the big Gerber in his right hand, waiting.

The captain lunged toward him. Frost made his style — they'd read the same books, practiced the same techniques and the man was good.

Frost stepped back into a classic knife fighter's stance. His feet were apart, not like a boxer's T-stance, but rather the toes squarely pointed ahead, the Gerber held in his right fist, point forward, his right elbow tucked against his right side, his left hand slightly out, ready to feign a move or go for a handhold. His knees were slightly flexed.

The fake commando captain was almost a mirror image.

"Come on, man!"

Frost smiled, not answering, moving slightly as the fake captain moved, edging, but never nearing the man. Neither of them was in reach of the other.

Frost feigned a lunge with his knife, the man sidestepping, starting a downward cut which, if Frost

170

had made the lunge, would have severed his brachial artery on the inside of his elbow — loss of consciousness almost instantly and unremitting death in under two minutes.

But Frost pulled back, flipping the knife into his left hand, feigning another lunge, the fake captain laughing, recovering and making a lunge of his own. Frost's right hand snaked behind his back to the little boot knife. He underhanded it across the six feet or so of airspace separating him from the fake British commando, the double edged, spear point blade hammering into the man's left breast.

The "captain" stepped back, staggering, looking down at the knife in his chest, then at Frost's face, his head shaking slightly from side to side.

He lunged forward, half falling, his knife missing Frost by a foot or more. Frost let him fall into the sand.

Frost started for his little knife, but never made it. Two men coming at him in a rush, Fairbairn-Sykes type knives in their hands. Already half stooped over, the one-eyed man scooped up a handful of sand, hurtling it toward the two men, catching one of them in the face.

Frost lunged forward, the tip of his knife penetrating the nearer, temporarily blinded man's radial artery in the left wrist as the man extended his hand to blunt the knife thrust. Frost spun away, kicking sand toward the second man, sidestepped as the man lunged. Frost wheeled, the first man going down, dying.

Frost slashed with the big knife in his right fist, opening a wound just above his opponent's right knee, then drawing back, recovering as the man cringed under the sting of the blade.

Frost rolled, another attacker starting for him. The one-eyed man caught up the Fairbairn-Sykes knife from the sand when the just dead man had dropped, then snaked it forward.

It was a clean miss. The attacker slowed though, sidestepping and Frost hauled himself to his feet, snapping out his right foot as he wheeled left, but feigning only, dropping to his right foot and snapping out with a kick with his left, catching the man in the right hip, throwing him off balance.

Frost stopped, snatched up a rock twice the size of a housebrick and hurtled it downward, striking the man in the face.

The man fell back.

Frost made for the fake captain's body again, getting it rolled over completely this time, wrenching out his little knife, then back-stepping as a man started for him. Frost dodged, turning, running back a step, then lunging, but only feigning.

The man made a broad sweep with his knife, Frost ducking under it, turning, catching the knife arm against the blade of his little knife, letting the force of the man's own thrust make the cut. Frost's right hand twisted round, then hammered back, the big knife hammering into the man's abdomen.

Another man was charging him, Frost letting the last man drop back, off his knife blade as he parried a thrust with the smaller blade in his left hand, then rammed the knife in his right hand forward, cutting into his new attacker's abdomen.

Frost started forward, no new attackers coming for

him, but the general fighting between his own force and the first landing party going on.

But these were Greek gunrunners and Sicilian Mafiosi—and their knife skills had been good, excellent, better than any of these men, hapless professional soldiers and would-be fighting men could have learned. Their knife skills—the Mafiosi and the gunrunner's men—had been ingrained since child-hood.

Ari had three men coming at him, and was handling two nicely, Frost thought. Frost raked the third man across the back of the neck, the drag against his blade making him think he'd severed the spinal cord. The man's body flopped instantly to the ground.

Kalantos was rolling in the sand with one man, a second trying to smash Kalantos' head with a massive rock.

Frost launched a half round kick into the man's left kidney with his right foot, then another, then another, the man dropping the rock, wheeling around, but Frost's right hand snapping forward, the point of his big knife cutting into the carotid artery.

Frost turned his face away as the blood spurted outward.

He spotted Alfonso, three men closing on him.

The one-eyed man ran, slicing a man coming for him across the adams apple, sidestepping the falling body, then reaching one of the three men going against Alfonso. Frost snapped his left foot out, into the coccyx, the tailbone, the attacker's body twisting around, the knees buckling. Frost fell on him with the knife, raking a jagged wound from the left shoulder blade down across the spine and into the right kidney.

Frost rolled left as he felt something coming for him, scooping up a handful of sand, hurtling it upward as one of the fake commandoes thrust for him, missing. Frost snapped up his left foot, catching the man in the groin, then rolled.

The one-eyed man was on his feet as the Chapmann man found him again, slicing at the air, Frost sidestepping, backstepping, backing away from the charge, looking for an opening.

Frost found it, snapping a hard kick with the toe of his right foot into the man's left rib cage, wheeling the rest of the way around, snapping a kick with his left foot, missing, but as the man recovered lunging with his own knife. Frost's knife blade bit deep into the left cheek of his attacker.

The man screamed, hacking the air with his knife as Frost ducked, snapping his right foot up and out, supporting himself on his hands, his right foot catching the man again in the groin.

The Chapmann commando fell back, rolling into the sand and Frost ran two steps then kicked the man in the right temple with his right foot, then again.

Frost wheeled, the knife in his right hand still dripping blood. There were muted screams, but the fighting was over and Frost closed his eye, the moonlight so bright now as the clouds parted that he could have counted the bodies. If he'd had the stomach for it.

Chapter Thirty-Six

Frost lay in the rocks again, sweating, cold, but not because of the night and the coolness of the air. The other men, experienced killers all, were staring down into their hands, or staring up into the sky—but none of them looked at one another, the one-eyed man observed. The killing. It had been the killing and the realization that soon—he glanced at the watch on his wrist, read its black luminous dial—it would start again, but this time with guns. The force would be too large to fight silently.

Nine of the impromptu commando band of Mafiosi and gunrunners had been killed, six more severely injured. One man, despite the morphine shots, still moaned in the darkness and each moan sent a chill up Frost's spine. The man had lost his left eye.

Frost sat bolt upright, hearing the change in the pattern of the lapping sounds of the waves against the shore. Rubber boats were coming.

Frost glanced up over the rocks. There were two hundred of the men, starting in toward the shore and for the operation to work, they must all die, he knew.

Frost checked the rifle in his hands—mechanically, absently, as if the hands belonged to someone else. He almost wished they did. It was not combat, not anything short of slaughter and now the second, the greatest chapter of it had to go on.

He would fire the first shots—that had been agreed upon earlier.

The one-eyed man twisted around, feeling the sand under him moving. He got to his knees, wanting it to end quickly. Thirty-five men with automatic rifles and the heartlessness to use them could kill two hundred men clamboring out of rubber boats, not expecting resistance to a clandestine landing.

You took out the forward security elements first, because those were the only ones ready to use their guns.

He sighted under the scope, not needing it at the range and not wanting to risk the light gathering qualities at night.

Frost eyeballed the nearest of the security personnel, watched him move out as part of a fanning formation, toward the rocks. Frost felt with his thumb around the pistol grip, moving the selector from safe to auto, then settling his thumb back in place around the CAR-16's pistol grip.

The first finger of his right hand twitched—a three round burst, the butt of the collapsible stock recoiling against his shoulder, the flat thudding sound of the FMC 5.56mms sounding in the otherwise total stillness like somebody dropping a safe three times.

Suddenly, Frost's ears rang, guns on both sides of him going off, assault rifles and submachineguns, the men going down in the waves, going down and falling over the sides of their rubber boats, the boats themselves exploding in rushes of air, men screaming, firing, bullets pinging against the rocks.

Frost tucked down, a full auto burst coming too close to him and the rock chips tearing into his left cheek. He felt the blood with his left hand, wet, sticky, and he could almost smell it.

Then he felt a smile crossing his lips. The killing was on the head of Eva Chapmann, the Deathwitch. He turned, started firing and cutting down her would-be mass murderers, head shots, gut shots—killing.

After what seemed an eternity but might have been less than a minute, Frost, Kalantos and Alfonso and Ari and some of the others started out across the beach, their automatic weapons blazing into the surf, Frost half stumbling into the waves as a corpse floated against his knees, firing out a thirty round magazine in his assault rifle, cutting down four more of the Chapmann mercenaries.

He rammed a fresh stick home, firing, into the surging water, feeling a hand on his shoulder.

The one-eyed man stopped shooting. It was Kalantos, his voice, even, calm, fatherly. Frost then wished he had a father to talk to. "It's over—they are all dead, Hank."

"For this—for this I'll kill her," Frost rasped, his hands shaking as he tried to light a cigarette, the surf still washing—cold—into his combat boots.

Chapter Thirty-Seven

There would be British troops coming in moments. Gibraltar was, after all, only two miles square, Frost remembered, still standing in the surf, hearing Kalantos rasping into the radio set, seeing the Sikorski helicopters coming out of the night sky.

One stage remained. The helicopters would carry off all of the men alive and wounded, even the dead so they couldn't be recognized. All but one helicopter. It was the one armed with the M-60 machineguns, the one that would carry Frost himself, Kalantos, Alfonso and the big balding Greek, Ari. It would carry them toward the freighter called the *Desdemona Fate*. Frost smiled at the thought, his hands steadier as he lit another cigarette. Desdemona—he doubted he'd strangle Eva Chapmann with a kiss.

He glanced at the Rolex on his wrist. The operation had gone almost too well. In less than a minute, six hydrofoils would start from the freighters Kalantos had off shore, closing in on the *Desdemona Fate*, all of them armed with machineguns and two of them with torpedoes, like the old PT boats of World War II.

Once the *Desdemona Fate* was engaged, Frost and the others would arrive by helicopter to land aboard the ship if necessary, to fight their way through to get

Eva Chapmann.

The thought almost amused him. Men like Kalantos and the Don—men the world called evil, men like himself. They were risking their lives and/or the lives of their men, to kill something they considered unspeakably evil, the Deathwitch.

Frost sometimes wondered who the good people of the world really were? Men like Kalantos and the Don—himself? or the sanctimonious ones, the ones who labeled all killing as bad, all violence as sinful and acquiesced to tyrants and usurpers, to mass murderers and lunatics. Were the inmates the ones who really ran the asylum?—as the old expression went, he wondered.

Frost could feel the salt spray pelting his face, drenching him now as the helicopter hovered over the beach, then started to land.

He looked to his assault rifle, changing the stick automatically, then working the safety on. He shouldered the rifle, diagonally, muzzle down, across his back.

The one-eyed man snapped his cigarette into the surf and started toward the helicopter. He was going to kill the Deathwitch and get the thing over—over.

Chapter Thirty-Eight

The whirring of the rotor blades overhead, the almost arbitrary clicks of automatic pistol slides being checked, rechecked. The sound of a fighting knife being edged against steel or stone.

Frost glanced beneath him—to the far west where the Rock of Gibraltar had vanished now behind him, there was purple darkness, but ahead of him, beyond the plexiglass of the helicopter's nose, there was a dull, almost warming glow. The sun was rising. Frost had sometimes through the night doubted that it ever would again.

The hydrofoils from Kalantos' ships had already engaged the *Desdemona*, a raging gunbattle in progress according to the fragmentary reports coming in over the helicopter radio set. And in the distance now, Frost could see the white puffs of explosions from a deck gun, and fire, the flames raging up from the center of a dark object on the horizon.

It would be the *Desdemona Fate*, Frost knew. His palms sweated, his fists balling—as the helicopter he was aboard drew closer to the naval battle below, he could see another helicopter, but smaller, the rotors idling, on the afterdeck of the *Desdemona Fate*. It would be Eva Chapmann's escape route. But this time, the one-eyed man whispered to himself, he would not lose her.

"Make a sweep on that helicopter there—shoot it up," Frost rasped through his headset to the pilot and the gunnery man. The pilot nodded, starting the Sikorski into a dive toward the decks of the *Desdemona Fate.*

There was a puff of smoke from the *Desdemona Fate,* and Frost could feel it in his stomach. "Missile," he shouted to the pilot, the gunnery man, then ripped the headset from his face and shouted to Kalantos, Alfonso and Ari—"There's a—"

The bubble of the helicopter shattered, the rotor blades above them veering off, away, the helicopter shuddering, lurching, then starting to drop like a stone.

Frost clawed at his seat harness, glancing behind him once. Kalantos was bleeding from the face and neck, Ari and Alfonso trying to get him out of his safety harness. "Jump for it!" the one-eyed man shouted, the waves hurtling up toward him, fire licking near his face and clothes with the plexiglass bubble gone.

Frost was in the open doorway beside the co-pilot's chair, then glanced back. Kalantos was up, stumbling and Frost grabbed for him, at the collar of his bush jacket, knotting a fist into it, then throwing himself from the plummeting machine.

His right wrist took the impact from the drag of Kalantos' body as he hit the water, the bone feeling like it was about to break. Frost slapped his left hand onto Kalantos' clothes and pulled himself and his injured friend under the surface.

His ears rang, pained—he wondered if they were bleeding. He could feel the explosion as the helicopter hit the water near him, the water surging around him, compressing him, driving the air from his lungs.

Kalantos' eyes were wide open, his hands clawing at Frost's hands holding him down. There was another shudder, Frost losing Kalantos, Frost's body pushed through the water like a fly slapped by a giant. His lungs burned, his head throbbed. Frost clawed toward the surface, oil slick burning on the water perhaps a yard from him.

The big Greek, Ari, was in the middle of it, screaming, thrashing in the water, his clothes on fire.

Frost sucked in air and dove, swimming under the oil slick, reaching up, the heat searing his skin as he dragged Ari down under the surface by his ankles.

The flames on Ari's clothes died and Frost hauled Ari through the water, clawing again toward the surface.

He could see the wreckage, sinking below the waves, see Kalantos in the distance, floating just above the water but moving, still alive. Frost dragged Ari, the balding gunrunner unconscious but breathing. There was no sign of Alfonso yet. Frost swam, to make it to Kalantos. Ari stirred once, screaming, fighting him. Frost crossed the big man's jaw with a short right, putting him out. The one-eyed man swam on, Kalantos starting to go below the surface, still too far for Frost to save.

"Signore! Signore!"

Frost craned his neck to the left, cursing the loss of his eye because he couldn't see without twisting half around in the water.

"Alfonso!" The Sicilian was swimming toward Frost, his face dark and scorched perhaps, or at the least oil smudged. "Take Ari—I'll get Kalantos—hurry!"

"Si!" Alfonso was coming, Frost's own strength flagging. In the distance, above the roar of gunfire from the fighting ships, he could hear a different sound. He looked toward it—one of Kalantos' hydrofoils was zooming over the water.

Ari was stirring again, but Alfonso was only yards away. "Hurry!" Frost shouted again, already starting to move through the water toward Kalantos.

Then Alfonso was beside him and Frost started to swim in earnest, his shoulders, his lungs, his ribs aching as he bent into a long crawl, the waves buffeting him. He looked up, seeing Kalantos' head just as it dipped below the surface. Frost sucked in air and dove, through the choppy waters seeing the shape of a man, starting to sink.

Frost swam on, Kalantos within reach, closer. Frost reached out, grabbing at the body, the collar of Kalanatos' bush jacket ripping away in Frost's hands as he grabbed for the man. Frost's lungs burned, his ears pounded with the beating of his heart, with his accelerated pulse rate.

Frost grabbed Kalantos by the hair and started pulling him up, getting his left hand onto the gunrunner's belt, dragging the man toward the surface. Frost broke his head through the waves, gulping air, feeling light headed, nauseated. He dragged Kalantos up, the Greek coughing, spitting, but breathing, however irregularly.

"Here! Here, captain!"

Frost looked up—a hydrofoil was within yards of him now, a boathook extending in the hands of a dark, muscular looking young man. More men stood in a knot around the man with the boat hook.

Frost reached out his left arm, his shoulders paining him as he did. He cupped the water in his hand, starting to drag himself through the waves. The boathook was reaching out to maximum extension.

"Here! Captain Frost!"

Frost shook his head to clear it, reaching out, water crashing across his face as he neared the hull. He closed his eye, shook his head to clear it, then reached out again. He could see Alfonso already aboard, he thought absently. Frost spit salt water from his mouth, stretching his fingers to maximum extension, just touching the tip of the boat hook, his fingers finding a purchase there.

"A little more," the one-eyed man rasped to his own body. He reached again, his left fist knotting around the wooden shaft of the boat hook. He could feel himself being dragged through the water and as soon as he felt the burden of Kalantos being taken from him, he closed his eye to rest.

Chapter Thirty-Nine

Nothing is perfect, Frost reflected. His plan to stop Eva Chapmann's precipitating a war between England and Spain over Gibraltar had succeeded. Kalantos was well, Ari was still recovering from his burns, but would survive. Only the helicopter pilot had died, even the gunnery man getting clear. And Alfonso was sitting outside the hotel suite bedroom, back on the job of guarding whoever the Don saw fit to guard.

But Eva Chapmann had escaped.

Frost closed his eye tighter, feeling the hands on his body. "You are tense — you must relax," Constanza whispered.

The one-eyed man smiled. "Relax — yes. I've got to do that."

"Open your eye — my cyclops."

Frost looked at her and laughed. She was straddling him, kissing his shoulders and chest. He touched the tips of his fingers to her breasts and she leaned back. He could feel her hands on his ankles as he rubbed her, watching the movement of her body, of her abdomen. "Hank — ohh," she murmured.

Frost rolled her over, onto her back, then coming on top of her, slipping between her thighs. He wondered why he felt the way he did. There was happiness with the girl. For once he wasn't shot to pieces. He glanced at his watch. It was almost time.

"Don't go, Hank," she murmured as Frost came into her. She screamed once, a tiny scream, pleasant, happy sounding. He could never be in the Mafia, he decided. To confide in a woman was one of the truest expressions of love, he'd always thought. But that was against the code. The women, the children, they were never told.

"Hold me," the one-eyed man whispered, feeling her body moving under him, hearing the short, panting sounds of her breathing. He felt his body start to stiffen, hers as well. She screamed again, digging her nails into his back as he sagged against her, his breath coming hard as he shuddered and then closed his eye. . . .

"Signore?"

Frost walked naked across the room, opened the door and looked out. "It is time, Signore—we must go."

"All right, Alfonso," Frost nodded, closing the door again, then looking across the room. Constanza was half covered by a silk sheet, sleeping in the center of the double bed, her hair tousled, her face peaceful. Frost started to pull on his clothes, catching a glimpse of the Rolex as he did. Alfonso was right—it was nearly time . . .

Frost walked down the steps of the hotel into the blinding afternoon sun, glanced once at Alfonso and then reached out his hand. "My friend—'til we meet again, huh?"

"Si," the younger man smiled, shaking Frost's hand warmly.

Frost started to the curb. "Signore?"

"Yes?"

"After this—this thing, where do you go?"

Frost felt himself smiling, lighting a Camel in the blue yellow flame of his Zippo. "I should be going back to the United States. Some things to take care of, a girl who wants to marry me, an old friend who's gotten himself into trouble. I'll keep busy."

"You and me—we made a good team, I think."

The one-eyed man smiled. "I think we did, Alfonso." Frost took the few paces back to the steps and shook the younger man's hand again. "I think we did," he repeated. Then he started for the curb once more, the car waiting. He started to get inside, his luggage already loaded; he turned back to Alfonso and smiled, "Like they say in the movies—keep your nose clean, kid, huh?"

The one-eyed man didn't wait for an answer . . .

Eva Chapmann looked rather attractive, Frost thought, looking at her briefly through a crack in the double doors. On the run from the Spanish Government, the British Secret Service, the Greek Government and the Sicilian Mafia she still managed to keep herself well. Her hair was almost too red to be real, and though he couldn't see from the distance, he understood from Kalantos' sources that she had changed her eye color to brown with contact lenses. The clothes were the strangest, almost unnerving part—she was dressed in a modern habit of an American Catholic nun, the black veil only showing the front of her hair, a white dress that stopped just below the knee, low-heeled black shoes and a crucifix around her neck on a chain. She sat alone at the table in the small restaurant, the restaurant less than two miles from the hotel where Frost imagined Constanza still slept and Alfonso still stood guard.

And it was the one giveaway—real nuns almost never traveled alone. But she was alone, just another Sister come to Rome to perhaps catch a glimpse of the Holy Father, to see the wonders of the architecture and art. But the Don's men had learned she was putting together another mercenary force, trying to recruit members from the Italian Communist Red Brigade Terrorist organization. For what purpose, Frost didn't know, nor did he care.

She had been found easily enough—the Don's Mafia contacts had their fingers into the hotel business in Rome, and the restaurant, like many throughout the world, was owned by a Greek, a Greek who was distantly related to the recuperating Ari by marriage. It had been simple after that.

Frost leaned against the kitchen counter, checking the revolver in his hands. It had started life, he imagined, as a standard four- or six-inch blue Model 29 Smith & Wesson .44 Magnum. But the barrel was cut back to just in front of the ejector rod, making it less than three inches. The front of the trigger guard was cut away and a wide trigger shoe installed, smooth. The hammer spur was cut away completely, and the grips were heavily wrapped with tape, so heavily that the grip was almost too big for the one-eyed man's hands, but the tape giving the gun a spongy feeling that would be good during recoil.

He checked the cylinder. Six one-hundred-eighty-grain jacketed hollow points, but the hollow points wider, more gaping than any conventional .44 Mag round he'd ever seen from a factory. He was told to hold the gun firmly, since the recoil would exceed any standard factory ammo he had ever fired. He wore skin-tight black leather gloves, but they wouldn't help against the recoil, just against fingerprints.

He had wanted to wait for her until she got onto the street, but the Don had advised against it. Killing even a fake nun in the streets would have precipitated a mob reaction. It was best to do the job in the restaurant, then flee.

A car was waiting outside, tickets at the airport. And once the deed was done an "anonymous" tip would be tapped to the Rome police, revealing the true identity of the woman as Eva Chapmann, herself a wanted terrorist.

Frost still didn't like murder.

"All right," he whispered, pulling the fedora hat low over his face with the sunglasses hiding his face as well. He pushed through the double doors, but slowly, walking from the kitchen and across the restaurant floor. No one noticed him.

He stopped, less than a yard behind her chair. He watched the slender shoulders tense under the nun's habit, the movement of the veil as she turned around to face him.

"Eva," he murmured.

The woman stood up, quickly, her chair falling to the floor behind her. She backed from the table. "God bless you sir—you have me mistaken for someone else."

She was looking at the gun in his hand. So was

189

everyone else in the restaurant and other than the occasional sound of a hurriedly taken breath, there was no noise at all.

"You're Eva Chapmann—you're no nun, and don't mock God," Frost rasped.

"But you're wrong, sir—I'm Sister Mary Andrew from Racine, Wisconsin—that's in the United States. I teach fourth grade to educably mentally handicapped children."

"No—you're Eva Chapmann, the Deathwitch," Frost insisted, his guts churning. What if the Don and Kalantos had been wrong? What if she were really a nun? He couldn't take the chance, he thought. Not that.

"You're Eva Chapmann," he repeated, but the conviction gone from his voice.

"Ohh, sir—whatever it is that troubles you—you won't solve it with a gun. Please, put it down," and she dropped to her knees in front of him, her hands folding in prayer, her eyes upcast, her lips moving silently—praying?

"You're Eva Chapmann," Frost insisted, taking a step back, terrified that she wasn't.

"Ohh, young man—I beg of you to repent, to put down that gun. Violence is never the answer—please," and she started up from her knees, her hands still folded in prayer. Frost put the revolver's muzzle down, away from her body.

"Sister—I—" He was wrong—this wasn't Eva Chapmann, it was some horrible mis—

"Die!!!!!" The scream was inhuman, animal, but more than that, the knife blade in the clutched together fists six inches long, hammering down at him, the blade a strange, yellowing color rather than the color of steel. "Die!!!" She screamed it again and Frost swung up the muzzle of the .44 Magnum, firing.

One round—she stumbled back.

Two and three, the body spun, gaping holes in the abdomen, her body hammering against the far wall, blood smeared on the white dress in long, ragged dark lines.

"Frost—you bastard!" She lurched away from the wall, not really walking, falling, hacking with the knife and the one-eyed man fired—four, five, six, his ears ringing badly, the web of his right hand sore, aching, his right wrist feeling as though he'd sprained it fighting the recoil.

The nun's veil was gone as the body flopped to the floor—dead.

The one-eyed man stood beside her a moment, picking up the strange colored knife in his right hand—it smelled like—. It was, human excrement. Instant and almost always fatal blood poisoning.

He reached down and removed the crucifix from around her neck, not wanting to be part of the sacrilege that she should still wear it.

"Deathwitch," he murmured, dropping the gun to the floor and walking out.

GREAT BOOKS

E-BOOKS

AUDIOBOOKS

& MORE

Visit us today

www.speakingvolumes.us